Chloe had always had a passion for writing, when she was in school, English was her favourite subject. So, a few years later, she had an idea of a story and started writing it. She wanted to put her pen to the paper and create something that she could share. She currently lives in Essex with her twin sister and her two cats and is in the middle of writing the sequel to this book. She hopes she can continue to share more of her ideas.

I would like to dedicate this book to all my family and friends who believed in me. Your support means so much

Chloe Ladd

YOU, ME AND THEM

AUSTIN MACAULEY PUBLISHERS™

LONDON • CAMBRIDGE • NEW YORK • SHARJAH

A CIP catalogue record for this title is available from the British Library.

ISBN 9781035820276 (Paperback)
ISBN 9781035820283 (ePub e-book)

www.austinmacauley.com

First Published 2024
Austin Macauley Publishers Ltd®
1 Canada Square
Canary Wharf
London
E14 5AA

I would like to thank Austin Macauley Publishers for believing in my work and helping my dreams come true by helping my book reach publication. I will always be grateful for the opportunity and cannot wait for Camilla's story to be shared.

Chapter One

Here it is, 'Happy Friday' as some would call it; these kind of people obviously do not work as a high-class escort (not a whore) on the weekends.

I wish I could agree that it will indeed be a happy Friday but the only happiness I will be involved in will be the orgasmic screeches coming from Mr Duffy's 'happy ending'. I swear, that man loves a hand job, you tickle his balls and you're golden (much like 99% of the male population. A slight breeze in the right place is all they bloody well need). Easiest £500 I ever make.

As I leave the office of my mundane administrator job, this is all in my thoughts as he is the first client of the night. Oh yes, there come more. Sometimes, I can fit in five clients a night based on what their preference is. Lucky for me, some of the clients I meet are handsome and can engage in invigorating conversation as well as a good lay. These are the clients I look forward to.

Although, having said that Dr Jimbo (yes that is his actual name) is on the cards tonight after Duffy and though some might get thrills from pretending to dissect a man's body parts from head to toe wearing said man's doctors coat and name badge, I can't say it really does it for me. However, my god, does he pay well! £1,500 per session and I am not even joking. This man is clearly a secret narcissist...or an obvious one.

I am on the tube now heading south west. This is where all my clients seem to live which in retrospect makes perfect sense. Before too long, I am getting off the train at South Kensington and finding the nearest hotel where I can get ready for this evening's continued events (if there are any).

Mr Duffy has been wanked off to perfection and Dr Jimbo yet again has been able to envisage himself as a sexy brunette. A successful night for us all, I think!

As I am walking to the hotel, I will now spend the night in, a thought occurs to me (as it does almost every other weekend), I wonder what my parents would think? They are under the impression that I am an executive at my shitty little office in Waterloo. But the same conclusion I always come to whenever I think this is the successor. I don't really care what they think, living a lie makes my life more exciting, so I will continue to roll with it! My new note-to-self is to prevent this train of thought from leaving the depths of my deepest darkest confines in the future.

Oh, I almost forgot to mention, my name is Camilla Jones, and this is my life.

Chapter Two

Saturday morning, I am taking full advantage of the £2,000 I made last night and ordering from room service. I evidently think I can eat for a family of four from what I have ordered but hey, isn't that the point of room service? Splashing out on any fancy entrée you can find on the menu, hardly eating any of it and washing it down with a large bottle of red. Now, I clearly seem like a raging alcoholic after making that statement but don't worry, I only drank four glasses.

I stumble out of the hotel at around 11:30 am to seem more efficient to the hotel staff. This gives them a spare half an hour to clean up after me before the usual check out time of 12 o'clock. How thoughtful am I?

I have a bit of free time before I have to meet another client, Mrs Chiswick. I mean before you assume, let me tell you that money is money, and the sexual orientation of my customers doesn't bother me. If you must know, outside of work, I happen to be straight. I have had a couple boyfriends in the past, however, now with my new profession in tow, it's not really the best ice breaker on a first date…

"Hi, I am Camilla, and you may notice I am terribly busy and unavailable most (every) weekends due to the massive queue of horny men and women who pay me for my services.

On the plus side, I have a pet cat who can keep you company!" Somehow, I don't think the second part of that sentence will even get a chance to make an appearance once nice man Fred I met at the gym hears the first part and runs a mile.

Therefore, I am sadly boyfriend-less and do have a lovely cat companion back home called Bubbles as the stereotype stands.

I come across a Starbucks on my way back to my flat and cannot resist buying a tall caramel macchiato, decaf, of course, because I do not want that twitchy eye nonsense I have endured in the past creeping back. I do not need the caffeine; anyway, I am already full of energy.

My flat is in the east area, a long way from the clients but if I lived there I would draw too much attention to myself when I invite friend over. "How can a shitty admin job land you with a penthouse like this?" I can hear them wail at me. So, best to keep it nice and modest to be on the safe side.

I was always terrible at being put on the spot in school, having to answer so many questions about fractions and how many pears does Dave have if he eats two but has ten and gives three to a friend. My mum and dad come from humble origins, so I just tell them my flat is modest just like my upbringing was and I like it that way no matter what my pretend executive job could potentially provide.

Finally, I set foot on the pebbled street leading up to my flat and am thankful my home is only on the second floor. I am still less likely to get burgled on this floor which gives me a fair amount of comfort.

I put the key in the front door and turn it. As I step in, the smell of cinnamon is still in the air from my religious use of Yankee candles. I think I have at least ten in my flat and I light them every night I am here. I am surprised the smell hasn't choked me to death yet. Just as I set my bag down on the sofa, Bubbles comes running out of the bedroom. It's so nice to come home to a loyal cat who loves you unconditionally. I find her some food and place it on the floor in her food bowl by the fridge whilst giving her a loving stroke.

I get in the shower and clean myself up ready for Mrs Chiswick. The funny thing about this particular client is that she is married to a man but craves sexual exploration with women in her downtime. I am not one to judge, so good for her; she is fifty-five years of age and still finding herself. Her husband is a top-end banker, so you can imagine how well kept she is. They live in this massive house in Chelsea with a built-in swimming pool in the basement.

I have been told to be at the house by 4:00 pm which is an hour before her husband finishes work. I put on my best Baywatch swimsuit and pull over a nice pair of black skinnies, a black top and red heels. I think you can probably guess why the swimsuit is needed but I will let your mind wander a bit.

Yes, you guessed it, her secret obsession is with Pamela Anderson in the Baywatch years. Her preference is that I turn up, meet her down in the swimming pool dressed as a lifeguard. I then jump into the water to save her from her fake drowning and finish it off with a bit of fingering. She reaches her climax and then we shower together. I never let her touch me because as I mentioned earlier, I'm not into women. She then gives me a hefty envelope as we are drying off full of fifties. I reckon I make at least £3,000 off her and I love it. Rich, lonely wives are ones to look out for.

Chapter Three

I try to keep Sundays as free as possible so that I can spend time with friends. If I am unavailable every weekend with no boyfriend, questions will emerge, and I haven't got time for that. So, usually on a Sunday, I meet my two best friends from school, Jack and Stacy. I do not know how I have been able to keep my newly positioned side job out of our drunken conversations, but I am doing one heck of a job so far! We usually meet at Bad Egg in Barbican which obviously is a terrible name for such a delicious restaurant.

The three of us order cocktails and breakfast and spend the afternoon chatting away. Being the only single friend out of the bunch I think they have stopped asking me the dreaded "are you seeing anyone?" question out of pity. We say our goodbyes at around 3:00 pm and head on home to enjoy the rest of our Sunday evenings.

When I get home, I light all my ten cinnamon candles and run a relaxing bath. I need to prepare myself for the shitty job I unfortunately spend five days a week at and this is my Sunday ritual. I honestly do not understand how people cope with just one job as boring as this and not want to cry themselves to sleep every night! Or maybe that is exactly what they do.

My alarm goes off at 7:00 am and I am already dreading work. I wonder how much longer I can keep this façade up. I need to make enough side money so I can jet myself off to the Bahamas for a lifelong holiday where I will never have to look at a computer screen or irritating bobby's face from accounts ever again. A girl can dream, right?

Why does it always feel like you are wasting your life in an office? You sit at a computer all day and try your best to not fall asleep at the sheer boringness of it all and get your arse fired, this in itself is a job.

The clock hits 12 o'clock and I am sending my work colleagues the mandatory 'out for lunch' email. Annoying Bobby who I previously mentioned insists that he too take his lunch at 12 o'clock and that we should go together. This happens every day without fail, hence the label I have now given him. Me not wanting to be rude, I kindly oblige every time.

We take our pick from the row of sandwich shops and decide to go with *Pret a Manger*. Their food is good, but their coffee tastes like soil without a load of syrups thrown in. I might give them the heads up one day.

Bobby and I pick up our sandwiches of choice and grab a coffee each. Once we have paid, we decide to be a bit adventurous and eat in rather than take it away only to go and sit back in our office. Wow, we are definitely living life on the edge today.

Whilst I take a bite out of my cheese ploughman's, Bobby decides to engage in casual conversation with me. He babbles on about his wide range of diet regimes and how he has tried them all but cannot seem to stay in shape. By this point, all I can hear is blah blah blah because the thing about Bobby is, he is an attention seeking wanker. His body is in terrific shape; he is just fishing for compliments as per usual or an offer to go to the gym with him, so he can perv on me whilst I squat. I do get so sick of his shit; however, the best way to manage a happy (bearable) working life is by pulling out the friendship card to whoever will take one. At this rate though, I believe this is his ten thousandth card. I am running out of cards; 'Bobby, stop taking them you selfish git!'

Lunch comes to an end finally and we walk (stroll) back to the office side by side. I think at one point Bobby brushed his hand against mine in an attempt to hold it…no chance, pal! This has not been a date, stop trying your luck. I sigh in disbelief at his poor attempt of reading my signals yet again. I miss my cat.

Chapter Four

'Buzz, Buzz' I hear my phone vibrate. It's Thursday morning about 5:00 am, which is too early in any world where people enjoy sleep. I haven't got to get up for work yet, so I am contemplating murdering this person who thought it was a good idea to text me at this ghastly hour. I unlock my screen, trying not to impair my vision I put the screen brightness all the way down. I tap the open message button, ah, it's from Claude. Let me give you the lowdown on Claude Blanc.

He is this beyond sexy Frenchman from Cannes in the South of France whom I met last summer on my 'working holiday'. This trip was a business trip but of course pleasure comes into it seeing as I am a high-class escort. Business and pleasure is always mixed in this line of work and I thank god, every day for the opportunity. So, anyway, I was assigned to be Claude's date to a special charity event he was invited to. A lot of men pay for a pretty woman to be by their side for such things.

When I first laid eyes on him I think, I orgasmed right there and then. He hadn't even touched me at this point, so you can imagine how appealing he was. He was the equivalent of a box of Krispy Kreme doughnuts smothered in cream with a box of the finest macaroons you could ever find thrown in the mix, also covered in cream. That is my idea of heaven, you guys. He was so yummy, I even considered cannibalism for a quick moment. Don't worry though, I didn't do that. Why would I want to spoil that enticing face of his that I would love to sit on?

What he is hiding underneath is also more than worth it I can assure you and I made a conscious effort to stick around to see it if it killed me. I made my way over to him, putting on my best sexy voice as I greeted him. We exchanged kisses on both cheeks and then I took his arm as we entered the events hall.

That night was so much fun! Not only was he sexy as hell, he was charming, smart and funny. I most definitely fancied him and could not wait for the second part of my services to begin.

He was staying at a nearby hotel, so we made our way to its reception and collected our room key. I was already wet from the anticipation. Room 301 was ours, the deluxe suite. Ah, Claude, you shouldn't have (no you really should have)! I put my bag down and shimmied my way over to where he was standing. I reached for his belt but before I could get to his zipper, he stopped me. I was so confused I'm not going to lie…I hoped and prayed he wasn't one of those wealthy closeted gay men that only wanted to save face. Luckily, for me though, he wasn't. He whispered in my ear, "No, you don't have to do anything. I will make love to you in exchange for your company, offering my male services to you instead. I hope you don't mind, Cherie." I will also not lie, when I heard that I thought, result! It won't be him on his back tonight for a change!

And there it is, the beginning of our love story. Well, not quite the love part but it was definitely the start of a remarkably interesting week full of fun in the sun and plenty of sex, chocolate and wine. Oh, how I wouldn't mind being there again now. It is currently pissing it down here in London and I still haven't managed to invest in some wellies. The thought of my shoes squelching away whilst I walk gives me the shivers.

Anyway, back to Claude and his text message which reads, "Mon, Cherie, I have been thinking of you lately and would love it if you would come visit me in France this weekend. If you say yes, your flight is already paid for. I hope to hear from you soon. Claude x" Ermmm, let me think about that one…stay at home and pet my pussy all day (and by pussy, I mean Bubbles, duh), waiting for a client to call me or spend the weekend in France with the epitome of sexiness and charm? Fucking hell, Camilla, it isn't difficult! Why pet your pussy when someone else can do it for you?

I cannot focus on work today as I am too overcome with excitement and anticipation for this weekend with Claude. Bobby tries to talk to me all afternoon; this time about his night boating hobby and how I should come along. I mustered up enough strength to let him down gently and carried on daydreaming.

It's a shame the weather is shit both here and in France, so we cannot relive our gorgeous summer together. I will however conjure up a plan that makes up for that.

The good thing about winter though is that you can use the old layering technique. The idea is to wear just enough layers to shield you from the cold and make sure your stockings and suspenders are intact. The wrong take on layering would be to wear too many clothes…the conclusion to that unearthly mistake would result in him being too exhausted to fuck you. No, no, no, we do not want this to happen. No man enjoys unwrapping a present with never ending wrapping paper it's that simple. We would rather they left the Stanley knife and scissors at home for this interaction.

Just as I engage my interest (somewhat) back into the conversation with Bobby, I can't help but think that there is something quite creepy about boating in the dark.

Chapter Five

It's Friday evening and Gatwick Airport is seemingly very busy. I have checked myself in and am awaiting my departure at 8:00 pm. Sitting down eating my double cheeseburger from Burger King is extremely pleasing to the taste buds. I know what you all must be thinking, you are all thinking of how much you too want to be eating a double cheeseburger right now and may be tempted to buy one. I say yes to the cheeseburger! Whoever says they don't eat meat, cheese or bread mustn't have a very fun life…that being said, I hold no real judgement and didn't really mean that comment. I highly suggest that vegan and vegetarian options should also be given a chance.

Goodness, I am such an all-rounder, why does my cat not appreciate this? I have purposely fed her all of the above just so she can be versatile if there comes a day when one of these options is no longer available. Unluckily for me, Bubbles is a stubborn meat-eater not capable of change (yet). This is not over…

I finish the last bite with glee and get myself to the gate. Ah, Claude is such a doll, he's of course paid for me to fly first class even though this journey is under an hour. Hey ho! I am not complaining. Free champagne coming my way is my idea of a good time, especially if it keeps on coming. I have this amazing skill when it comes to alcohol. I can drink a lot more than I should be able to for my size and this unquestionably helps me out with the clients who have an insatiable thirst for liver poisoning.

I have finally reached my destination. After that lengthy forty minutes to Paris, I must have consumed at least half a bottle of champagne. The weather has brightened up a bit and by that, I mean it has decided to stop raining. This probably won't last very long as my iPhone weather app says there is a 100% chance of rain for the next decade. I follow the queue of people to the baggage area and then remember I only needed the hand luggage that I already had in my hand and thought to myself I should probably drink less before I lose my mind completely.

I trotter my way on to the exit where my car will be waiting for me but then out of nowhere, I find myself on the floor. Of course, I missed the wet floor caution sign. I gather my composure and start to get up from the wet patch that has now stained my bottom and suddenly feel a pair of hands on me. As I turn to meet the eyes of this kind citizen, I freeze. He was tall, around 5'9ish I'd say. He had brown hair and the bluest eyes I have ever seen. They were like little pools of ocean staring right at me, making me wish I were swimming in them. Once he had got me to my feet he threw a cheeky wink at me and said "Better watch where you are going next time aye. Not gonna lie though, your bum still looks fantastic!"

I throw my cheekiest smile his way and thank him for his help however, I would like to know his name.

The next thing I know he does just that, introduces himself. He must have read my mind. "The name is James Splinter and you're welcome love." He walks away and I endeavour to find the nearest toilet so I can dry my wet bottom before I meet Claude. I should still have some time.

Halfway through this process, I get a text from him, just typical. He wants to know where I am. I dab my bum for one last check and it seems dry enough. As I locate the car, the door swings open and Claude greets me. He is just as delicious as I remember. Now, I am sure you know how it goes when you have your own personal chauffer. They are on your payroll and therefore whatever you choose to do in the backseat is not their concern. Due to this, I find myself on my knees and what follows is a pukka blowjob. In all car situations, it is important to keep the leather seats free from liquid damage. Do I need to spell it out for you? I don't think so.

I bet you are all wondering what I have been up to over the weekend. Well, I can assure you that in between sex, sleep and more sex, we did get out a fair bit! You see, people probably assume that an escort just humps and dumps the client as soon as sex is over, but I am here to put those assumptions to rest as I am NOT a hooker. Part of the reason why escorts are so successful is because there are a lot of people out there who just want some company and our job is to make them feel incredible regardless. On that note, women and men pay me just for that reason and that my friends is as PG as it gets.

Moving on, Claude kindly wakes me up that morning with a box at the end of the bed. Let's hope it's not a severed head, otherwise I will no longer be meeting his acquaintance. Turns out though, that when I open it, what's inside is a beautiful gold gown with a note placed delicately on top of the glorious fabric.

I tear open the envelope with no hesitation because this gown is not going to explain itself. It reads, "Camilla, I would be honoured if you would wear this by my side as my escort (pun intended) to a ball I must attend. Meet me outside the hotel at 7:30 pm, Claude." Well, well, well, looks like I have a ball to attend. God, I love my job.

7:30 pm is beckoning and I am just finishing off my hair and make-up. This dress is right up my street, fitted and hugging my curves in all the right places. Right on cue, I receive a text message from Claude telling me he is outside. I was a good girl and only had two glasses of wine before I departed the hotel room.

When we arrive, I am thankful that there are no visible photographers waiting to pounce. I understand that I am in a different country however, I do not wish to take any chances. Imagine my photo turning up in the *Daily Mail* or something, 'closet escort is revealed to the world!' hmmm, no thank you. I bet you annoying Bobby would be all over that…Jesus, where is the champagne?

Claude pulls me out of my reverie and introduces me to a couple hundred people, all who work with him in one way or another. I am just about to shake hands with Dr talks a lot when someone catches my eye from the corner of the room, and by room, I mean the French Buckingham Palace.

Where do I recognise this man from? I most certainly haven't slept with him yet. Omg! It's wet bum guy from the airport. I make up an excuse to go and speak to him by insisting I get Claude another drink. As I strolled over, there it was, a sickening feeling in my stomach like butterflies. I stopped in my tracks to regain my composure for the second time this weekend. What is wrong with me? Oh, damn it, he's only gone and decided to meet me halfway, gracing me with his presence.

"I know you. You are the lady from the airport who had that wet bum incident!" I must have composed myself because my response was as witty as ever.

"Ah, yes, and you are the gentleman from the airport who has a surname representing a painful injury caused by playing with too much wood."

He laughed quite energetically at this so I knew he understood. "Yes, my dear, that's me. Mr Splinter, well done! I am going to let you in on a little secret about me missy. It's not just a name, I am fully trained in getting those little bastards out of your skin, so if you ever need me to get under your skin, I would be happy to assist."

Okay, is he actually charming or is this the cheesiest shit you have ever heard? Either way I find myself soaking it right up somehow. Should I see a psychiatrist? WHERE IS THE CHAMPAGNE?

Unfortunately, the delightful encounter is interrupted by an intrigued Claude who by now probably thinks his date had been abducted. He shakes James's hand and puts a protective arm around my waist as they exchange pleasantries. Once that is all done and dusted, Claude and I bid James a due (I am not so happy about this decision).

The clock strikes 12 o'clock and Claude is putting his hand up my skirt under the table, I think he is getting a bit antsy and I suspect his growing hard on is getting a bit much to bear at this point so we get up to leave the hall.

When Claude is restless like this, he just wants to get in and get out as soon as possible but I am just not feeling it at all. Truth be told, whilst he is hurling his body on top of mine, all I can think of is that twat Splinter. I know his first name is James but I will use this as my nickname for him. Oh god, I am giving a man I barely know a 'pet name' already? How endearing of me. No, what the actual fuck! I try to bring my psyche back to the intercourse I am currently engaged in.

I get back into the mood and switch roles with Claude. I climb on top of him and position my pussy tight around his dick and ride him like a motherfucker. I speed up my tempo and clamp my nails into his chest leaving indents in his glorious skin. He is loving this and begs me to scream his name. I would usually do this for a client no problem, but right now it feels wrong. God help me if Splinter is the reason for this. Oh shit...

The next morning is my final day here in Paris and I thought I would wake up in my hotel room by myself. But oh contraire, Claude is STILL here. This is not typical behaviour for him on my previous visits, so I am slightly concerned about what is going to happen when he wakes up. Twenty minutes later, he awakes and gives me a sexy smile. Usually this would make me melt but not this time.

"Mon, Cherie, I have been meaning to discuss some things with you. By far, you are my favourite escort and I enjoy the time we spend together. Last night, seeing you flirting with that other man right in front of me, I was wild with jealousy. I did not want it to continue any longer and so this is my question to you. Camilla, will you please stop seeing your other clients? I do not want another man touching you. I will pay you to be mine and only mine." Woah, hold on there, Frenchie, this is not how it works. If I want to be exclusive with a client, I call the shots. He may be the epitome of sexiness but I do not want this at all. Best believe I was on the next available flight out of Paris.

Chapter Six

So, it turns out my previous assumption that caffeine is the reason why I get twitchy eye syndrome was well off. I have had no caffeine at all for weeks and then bam, this Monday morning it hit me like an epileptic fit. My eyelashes were all over the shop! The mystery continues…

I have googled other possible causes for this and my findings were zero help to my predicament. I went to the opticians a month ago and they told me my vision was 20/20 and I am not consciously stressed right now. That narrows it down to eye-strain which I could totally believe because the computer screen I stare at on a daily basis has no consideration for my retina. I'll put this to the side for now as I am still struggling with the concept.

After a long day of debilitating eye twitching at work, I thought I'd pay the local gym a visit. The thing with me is I can lose weight by just eating less and a bit healthier which is obviously a positive thing especially in my line of work. However, even though my love for sleep and lounging around is unbreakable, I do actually enjoy working out when I do it and I wish that I had a gym in my apartment.

This would be the best thing ever as I wouldn't have to leave the house to hop on the bicycle! This is where I decide to buy an exercise bike. What are they going for these days? £50 seems relatively cheap, that'll do. This is my mental note whilst I am tugging on the rowing machine. I will add this contraption to the list too but once I work out where I can put it.

So, an hour done in the gym and I am ridiculously horny. I have no clients tonight to my disappointment (though it is a weekday). I scan the gym for eligible men to fuck and notice a tall blonde entering the steam room. I follow him. I shut the door behind me and he looks at me with a mixture of lust and confusion. He has no idea I am about to sit on his dick but this makes it more exciting for me anyway.

I walk over to him holding my finger to my lips gesturing to him to keep quiet. I remove his towel and have a look at the goods. Impressive, I must say. This gives me the urge to get on my knees and start this off with a bit of foreplay. I do love a cock in my mouth at the best of times. He seems to be enjoying this as I can feel his erection growing in my mouth. I can get wet just by sucking some dick so were both ready for the next move.

I get up, place myself on top of his massive hard-on and slowly move up and down, teasing him a little. He lets out a bit of a moan and then I speed up. This frustration needs to end sooner rather than later. We both moan some more and he's kissing my neck now which pushes me over the edge. By this point, we are both sweating like crazy, literally dripping. I feel him exploding inside of me and am thankful because I had already managed to cum three times. I ease myself off from him and pick up my towel. He is about to attempt conversing with me; however, I am out of the door before he can mumble his name.

I get home and Bubbles runs up to me straight away offering a loving purr and nuzzles my leg. I wish it were a nice man waiting for me sometimes but she doesn't need to know that. I still very much appreciate the level of comfort she offers me. I wouldn't mind it if that James Splinter were in my bed every night, there is something about that one. I can't quite put my finger on it.

Once I have settled my things down I throw myself on my bed, I'm still thinking about James. I have the urge to reach down into my knickers and have a little play. Visions of his cheeky wink and how his hands felt on me at the airport enter my mind. I'm just a young woman with a high sex drive that plagues me and all I can do about it is masturbate.

It's been another dry week with the lack of clients in the areas I need them to be in but rather than fuck anything (like I did in the gym), as exciting as that was, I don't need to make a habit of acting like a nymphomaniac on the prowl. I decide to branch out myself and look for new clients.

How I decide to do this is to go out every night after work and see whose game for some paid fun. I will not accept unpaid sex again unless I get a boyfriend. Slim chance of that, so I should have no problem raking it in! It's Thursday night and I have my LBD (little black dress) on, with almost sheer black stockings and my favourite pair of black stilettos. I would wear my red heels but that would look borderline hooker and that's not the vibe I want to give off, especially in this limited amount of fabric. Yes, I am aware I am a high-class escort but I don't need everyone in the bar to know that subtleness is key.

Luckily for me, all the girls in the bar are wearing similar outfits, so I don't feel out of place one bit. It's still cold here in the UK, so I am glad for the stockings keeping my legs warm but adding a sexy flair. The music in here is good, it's a mixture of R 'n' B and hip-hop and right now R Kelly is playing. It's obviously a good choice for me to end up here tonight seeing as this is setting the mood and all the men are looking around like they're ravenous for some interaction.

If I am being truthful, I am scanning the room for someone who resembles Splinter and this is when I realise I may have some feelings developing. I also now realise that I sound like a bit of a psycho in love. Oh no, this is not ideal. Not ideal one bit. He's not here though, so I will have to make the most of who is and remember why I am here.

I need to get my working girl head back in the game and so I rescan the room and decide to speak to a blond man called Sam, a ginger called Sebastian and an Italian looking Dolce. They are all flirting with me ridiculously and so I thought why not see if they would be interested in a four-way for £1,500 altogether, £500 each. They initially laugh at the price of the evening but then I let them in on my little secret and the convincing was no longer necessary.

I ask them all to meet me in the hotel upstairs, the Mayfair Hotel, but tell them to leave at separate intervals to draw less attention to the situation. Once all three are present in the doorway of the room I have booked for the evening, I gesture them all into the bedroom. I ask them all to strip down to their boxers and one by one I insist they drop them. I want to see what I am working with so I know how it should go down.

Ginger Sebastian is up first and he has a modest but strong looking cock, that's fine by me. Next is Blonde Sam, he has a slightly larger one but it's thinner. This is also okay with me as long as there isn't too much penetration on his part, thin dicks do not feel that good inside a woman, but it will do in the mouth or hand. Lastly, Italian Dolce. Despite his stupid name, his member is also perfectly adequate, quite like Sebastian's.

I am quite pleased with my choices and lay the cards on the table. I grab Sam's knob in my hand and start sucking. At this point in the transaction, I gesture for one of the others to do me from behind. Looks like Dolce takes the lead on that one. I feel his cock slowly slide into me and I can't help but gasp momentarily. He is in and starts pounding away. I get the feeling that he is going to cum first but then whoops, nope. It was Sam in my mouth. I swallow this with satisfaction and then he takes a seat. I let Dolce finish inside of me and then shuffle off of the bed to the bathroom.

I freshen up for Sebastian and get the other two to leave, taking my £1,000 as they go. I normally do all of the work seeing as this is what the service requires however I wanted to kill two birds with one stone with Sam and Dolce. I liked Sebastian the best. When I enter the bedroom once again, he is lying there on the bed waiting for me. I smile at him and make my way over to where he was.

I crawled on top of him and started riding him. This is my personal favourite position because it gives me the best orgasms out of the rest. I can feel his lips on my neck and this is turning me on even more. I pick up his hands and place them on my breasts. As he fondles away, I can see his facial expression changing. He is about to cum, I can tell. I throw my head back in pleasure and we both orgasm simultaneously. I am well and truly spent.

I went to get up but felt a hand on me. Sebastian looked at me with a curious look. "What's the matter?" I ask.

He smiles gently and then replies "I am just curious, why would a beautiful woman like you be paid for sex with strangers? You don't come across cheap to me despite what has happened here in this hotel room, why hasn't a handsome fella picked you up yet?" What a sweetheart he is. I knew there was a reason I preferred him to the others.

"Sebastian, I appreciate what you are saying to me, it really is lovely. I guess I just haven't found a man who was ever okay with me being an escort. I wouldn't do this if I had a man's feelings to think about but there just isn't one. I do have a normal job too by the way." He laughs at this and keeps quiet for the remainder of the time he has left with me.

When I am alone again, I start to mull over what he said to me. I love this job; it gives me a different life to live. However, since meeting James, my outlook on life has had a bit of a stir. I haven't been romantically or emotionally attracted to someone in what seems like years and two interactions with this man has made me loopy with wondering 'what if'. This is definitely the night my feelings for James were confirmed. But what do I do with these feelings over someone I am never going to see again? Life sucks right now.

I originally planned on staying at this hotel tonight but I decide to take a long walk home instead. I haven't felt this feeling of longing for quite some time. There I was, minding my own business, fucking for money and loving it, the next thing I know, some loser charms the pants off me and I'm a broken woman! Usually, having three men in one night of my choice (which is nice) would be enough to have me flying high on cloud nine. Looks like three cocks won't do...

I realise how stupid it is to walk this kind of distance on a wine-filled stomach; however, I am an escort on a mission! I pass all the clubs, bars, pubs in the district with at least one or two men trying to get me to go home with them. Sorry, guys, been there done that, three times. It starts to get a little chilly out, I feel like I need the air but I am not even halfway to my flats postcode before I give up and signal at the nearest taxi. At least I can leave the window wound down so the air can still circulate. The taxi driver tries to make small talk but I am just not in the mood so I think the message is received.

You see, this is why I hate feelings. The minute you catch them, you're a goner! Ah, I finally start seeing the surrounding area of my flats location and I couldn't be happier. I want to get home, get naked and watch a soppy film whilst eating ice cream. What a great plan, Camilla, you've turned into one of those girls.

Chapter Seven

I am awoken by the obscene sound of my morning alarm; Jesus, I must have fallen asleep in my ice cream induced coma. That sound needs to jog on though seriously. I hit the snooze button, not feeling up to a happy Friday at work. I am not hungover which is a plus though. I stay in bed for another ten minutes and give Bubbles a cuddle. She truly is a darling. I sense she is cottoning on to my depressed state because usually she is not awake and giving me attention at this ghastly hour. Whatever her motive, I am desperate for the comfort.

I know you're probably thinking I should talk to my two best pals about my lovesick condition however, I will ask you to please refer back a few pages…that is never a good idea. So, it's settled, I only have my cat to comfort me.

I trudge my way through the mindless queues of robots on the streets. I tell ya, Londoners are so serious. They all act like they are on a mission that is life or death and really, they are just on their way to work. It's like, Susan chill the fuck out! Obviously, Susan is just a name I've thrown out there but this lady powerwalking next to me does look like she could be a Susan.

I get into the office and try my best to avoid eye contact with annoying Bobby. This proves unsuccessful and oh behold, he's invading my personal space. He is a good-looking guy, don't get me wrong, unfortunately, he reminds me of a gnat. He just hovers around you, waiting to pounce and sooner or later he is going to suck the very blood from your skin. The worst thing about these creatures is that they are silent fuckers. You're lucky if you see them coming.

In this instance, I didn't see him coming, he just manoeuvred his way halfway across the office to pester me. Draining my very existence. He asks me how my evening was and I cut him off short with a quick and snappy lie. "I was at home, watching *Saw 2*, great film that." He looks somewhat bemused by my response. This is my cue to make a quick exit. Well done, girl.

The afternoon takes a positive turn when I receive a text from the 'other' office. I didn't mention earlier who I worked for but I'll tell you a little background history. Madam Featherly founded the escort service back in 2002 and it has successfully been bringing in business ever since. It has a very prestigious clientele and she prides herself on this. I stumbled into this job by reading an ad in the newspaper, I know, who reads ads anymore, right? However, there is a method in her madness because as I mentioned earlier, discreetness is key in this industry.

Anyway, long story short, I called the number on the ad and she asked me to attend an interview. I thought, fuck it, why not. She took one look at me and said I was perfect for the job. She then briefly explained the going rates for money made and she didn't need to sell it to me any further. I was well and truly sold. Money makes the world go round they say.

The text said she had a new client in mind for me and he was tonight's subject. His name was Rodney, worked in telecommunications by day and was obviously down for someone to bring some excitement into his life after having a job like that. God could not think of much worse give or take a few on the jobs I would never do list.

I was scheduled to meet him at his apartment at 8 o'clock sharp but I wanted to get there at least ten minutes early. Punctuality goes a long way whatever the situation. I knock on the door and wait expectantly for this Rodney fellow. After two minutes this little head pops round the door, shy guy huh.

Normally, they are the ones to watch, so let's guess what fetish this one is in to. Puppets? S&M? Feet? I do hope it's not the feet because I have a ridiculously sensitive pair which will score him a night in the nearest A&E department if touched inappropriately.

He says hello in the most sheepish tone and lets me into the apartment. First impressions, apartment is relatively normal. Bedroom on the other hand looks like the pages of a Marvel comic magazine in physical existence. Secret geek springs to mind. He asks me if I would like a glass of wine and obviously, my answer is yes. As he scatters off to the kitchen, I take in my surroundings. I hear him make his way back into the room and look up to greet him.

What I am greeted with ladies and gentlemen is a half-dressed Rodney in a loin cloth. Yes, that's right...I try to disguise my need to laugh by downing the glass of wine he has just given me. Oh boy, this is going to be a funny night. I am not entirely surprised by this; however, you can always expect the unexpected in this job.

"You can call me Hot Rod, Sugar," is his opening line. Ah, he has an alter ego (referring to his manhood I'm assuming) but of course! I start to pretend that I take him seriously and walk over to him. I stop and unzip my dress, letting it fall to the floor.

Now it's crunch time…I put on my best innocent girl act and ask him what he would like me to do to him. He groans at this and responds "get your naughty little arse into my red room. You have been misbehaving and need to be punished!" Ah right, he's read 50 shades of grey…excellent. I do as I am told and make my way out of the current room I am in, even though I have no idea where his red room of doom is (that rhymed ker-ching).

Just left of the kitchen, there is a basement door. Classic. As I am walking down the stairs, I look at the surroundings, colour scheme is a nice shade of red I must say. At this point, the loin cloth he is wearing doesn't even phase me, I'm more intrigued as to what is down here to be honest with you.

We reach our destination and boy, this is like the exact replicate of Christian Grey's red room, must be a super-fan or something. It's quite hard to get my head round this Rodney, he has a ridiculously boring job by day, is also a secret geek and a secret freak in the sheets by night. Somehow, those attributes do not seem to match in the slightest. It amazes me still that there can be so many layers to people's personalities. Shrek had a point.

He gets me to lay on the bed and bounds my wrists to the headboard. He then shuffles into a smaller room in the corner and I wonder what is coming at me in the next five minutes.

Bang on the fifth minute, in my line of vision is Rodney swinging into the room on some kind of rope and lands on top of me. Clearly also a fan of Tarzan, he then thumps his fists against his chest and starts making baboon noises. Yes, this is happening. I am bound to a bed with a man on top of me doing strange things. Don't worry, I have had stranger in my time you'd be happy to know. The best thing to do is expect the unexpected and then you'll always be prepared if a surprise hits you right in the face. At this point, though, I do query the duration of this as I do intend to have sexual relations with this man for a big buck in this century, not the next.

Just as I finish that thought yes, he starts to do something! He pulls down my knickers and spreads my legs. He then stares at my vagina for a couple moments and then dives right in. It's been a while since someone ate my pussy and he is surprisingly good at it. My clit is doing somersaults right now and I am in heaven. My fucking god, his tongue is so moist as he slips it in and out of me sporadically. I am getting close; I can feel it. I thrust my hips towards him, trying to rake in as much pleasure as possible and then I let out an uncontrollable cry. Next thing you know, Hot Rod is ejaculating all over my chest. Hang on a minute, he just came from going down on me? That is a first!

I see myself out of the house, picking up my cash by the door as I go. See, I told you, the shy ones are the ones to watch. I text the madam and fill her in on my experience with Mr Hot Rod and she is not surprised either. It did however make her night to know I had just been tarzaned!

Chapter Eight

Thank god for the freaking weekend, I say to myself as I wake up around noon Saturday morning. One of the single most enjoyable things for me to do in life is sleep. I kid you not if I could get paid for staying in bed I would be the first one in line for that job and it would be fucking awesome. Sadly, I get paid to have a cock in one or all of my holes at every available opportunity. Although, I do get to use a bed near enough 80% of the time, so it's close enough. I wish someone would make me a cup of tea right now. That's something I am going to have to train Bubbles to do. All in good time…I hope. Forever being the optimist is what you call that my lovelies.

Accepting that Bubbles is not quite at that stage yet, I totter out of bed and pop the kettle on. I hear my belly rumble and try to decide what I can be bothered to conjure up for my breakfast, or brunch as some would class it as this time of day. I narrow the choices down to omelette or beans on toast and endeavour to go with the omelette. Whilst the eggs are sizzling in the pan, I am now onto my second cup of tea. See, I treat tea the same way I do alcohol guys because there is no sense in having one of each per day, got to have at least two (hundred) of both.

I turn the TV on to find Jeremy Kyle is on ITV, brilliant. I can enjoy my brunch whilst poking fun at the inbred guests. I honestly do not know how Jeremy can take these bunch of wankers seriously because I don't think any other human being on the planet who is remotely normal can either. At least this one's got most of her teeth…now, that needs to be praised.

I zone out for a little while, a variety of thoughts running through my head all at once. Why hasn't Claude even attempted to contact me? Where the fuck am I going to find James Splinter and declare my love for him? Maybe I should give annoying Bobby a go. I wonder if Bubbles spoke what she would say to me? She'd probably tell me to do one.

Oh, sweet Jesus, I need a ploy to bump into him again. But how? Time to do some brainstorming. Where is the paper and stationery kept in this flat anyway for that matter? I need to write some options down. I really have hit rock bottom, creating a spider gram based on a bloke I have met twice, fuck me. Is this all worth it? Most probably not. Still, I am too far gone now.

I have made no success for forty minutes and then boom it hit me. Why don't you just get a private investigator to hunt him down, Camilla? This works usually in the movies. Only difference is, this is real life and I sound like a real-life psychopath. Still, he won't know that if I just randomly bump into him so this is where I'm heading. Desperation at its wits end.

After an hour, my PI has gathered enough information of James's whereabouts and I couldn't be happier. If you're wondering how I have access to a PI, I have my sources. Let's see shall we, he is 28 years of age, lives in south-west London

(Clapham to be exact), has no kids, no CCJS and no criminal record. This is all appears very ideal but hold that thought because he's a fucking copper. And do you want to know what his current assignment is? Shutting down escort services and arresting women caught in the sex trade. I may as well handcuff my bloody self! Oh, this is not good news. Trust me to fancy a guy who indirectly wants to dispose of people like me. As ludicrous as this may sound, I still want to pursue him. Fuck it, I have been hiding my secret life for decades now from my family and friends successfully and he doesn't have to find out either. My mission starts now. I jump in the shower, put together a sexy casual outfit and take a leap of faith.

Deciding it is less obvious, I drive to Clapham Common instead of getting the tube. No one visits their aunty Rita via London transport if they have a parking space available to them (obviously, my cover story). The satnav takes me to a side road opposite the station, which is accompanied by houses, so far so good. I park outside door number 69 as this is one of the only houses without a bloody driveway to block in.

James works on the high-street in some little carpenters as his 'day job' because he is undercover majority of the time slaying hookers and what not. I steer clear of this train of thought asap pronto though. I bet he looks fit in his police uniform…I leisurely stroll towards the high-street Starbucks which is across the road from the shop. I grab myself a latte and place myself by the window. Hopefully, my non-caffeine-related-eye twitch kicks in (or at least pretends to), so I can avoid my dignity going down the toilet. Sadly, this does not happen and I am really a 25-year-old woman stalking a man.

Gotcha! There he is in all his yumminess stepping out for a cigarette. I don't agree with smoking but this is not stopping me. I pick up my cup and walk out of the Starbucks exit, cross over pretending I am on the phone and that I do not see him standing there opposite me when, "Camilla! is that you or are my eyes deceiving me?" Jackpot.

"Oh, my goodness, James? Fancy seeing you here! Didn't expect you to live in the same area as my aunty Rita...what a delightful surprise." My sarcasm saves the day every time. "Ah, so you aren't stalking me then aye, Cam?" His use of 'Cam' would have landed him a punch in the face if he were anyone else, but again his charm consumes me.

"Stalking is a crime Mr, plus I haven't managed to fall into any wood as of yet so your services are not required."

"So, you remembered our little chat at the posh do in France then? Must have made a good impression on you, sweetheart."

I try to refrain from blushing at his cheekiness by dropping a bit of witty flanter. "I remember the level of visible wood was in short supply at that charity event, must have been hard for you to cope." This is also a subtle way of seeing if he is that way inclined.

You must be sure of these things. "Ha-ha! You are right there, girl, but this worked out in my favour seeing as wood is just for the workplace."

Okay, here is another reason why I fancy the pants off this guy, he understands my banter and wit like it's second nature to him. I would so let him cum on my face, is there somewhere private in that shop of his?

43

"Well, as lovely as it was to bump into you, James, I must bid you a due. Aunty keeps texting to see where I am! Maybe I'll see you around."

As I turn to leave I count to four, "Wait, Camilla, we should get a coffee sometime. Beats 'possibly bumping into each other' doesn't it, darl!" Now usually, I loathe when people shorten words like darling but this twat (as I often refer to him) is doing things to me so I let it pass. The cutting-the-conversation-off-short ploy works a charm when a man is already a bit interested so it's a win for me today!

I reply with a satisfying, "Sure, why not! Here is my number, you'll need that." He gives me a little smirk and then I'm off. I know he's checking me out as I walk up the high street so I wiggle my bum fiercely. You'll be getting a close-up of this bad-boy soon enough handsome.

As I park up outside, my flat my phone rings. It's Madam. She tells me that there is another new client on the horizon for tonight. Sweet! Time to make a quick buck. His name is Tony and I have been pre-warned that he is an enthusiast for fucking in public places. This does not bother me in the slightest as long as it is nowhere near Clapham!

Luckily for me, he lives in the north region of London, so time to get myself ready. He asks me to meet him at Hampstead Heath park right by the entrance. I am just approaching him on the pathway, he is tall as fuck. 6'5, I would say, tanned and dark haired with a manbun. I have to say I am not a fan of this hairstyle men seem to think looks good on them however each to their own I always say.

I was told to wear a skirt or dress for easy access so this also meant going commando. He was wearing a pair of grey jogging bottoms and a white t-shirt. I stop dead in front of him and he puts a hand up my dress. This fella wastes no time. He grins as he feels the moist opening of my vagina and then proceeds to stick a cheeky finger up there. I let out a small moan and involuntarily bite my lip. The contact feels good on my skin. Admiring the ever-growing pleasure on my face, he picks me up and I wrap my legs around him.

There is a bunch of trees just to our left and in no time at all, I am pressed up against one in a couple swift movements. He pulls his jogging bottoms down and his erection is fucking enormous! He enters me and then starts passionately kissing me on the lips. I can feel the bark of the tree rubbing against the small of my back revelling in the pleasure, I don't hear the passers-by. Too caught up in the moment, we both are too far gone to stop but whoever it was they were getting an insight into a real-life porno. As long as it wasn't the cops, they can sit back and enjoy, for all I care! In Tony's case though, I have no doubt that he was aware of the onlookers because he sped up with incredible force and I just couldn't bear it any longer.

We cum in unison and then turn around to see if we can catch a glimpse of our audience, oh Jesus, it was a couple of teenage boys. There they stood with their mouths wide open. All I could do was laugh and Tony seems to have the same idea. He takes my hand and we walk to the exit. "I don't even know your name," Tony says to me.

"It's Camilla."

"Great, Camila. I will give you your money in a short while; however, it is not here in this park. I have one other place where I would like to fuck you. Would you do me the honours?" I am not one for turning down seconds, so I kindly oblige. We get into his car and drive to the Southbank.

45

We park the car and he takes me to the pier. I think I know where this is going…he wants to fuck me on a boat in the middle of the Thames. I am down for that alright. He owns a boat, so we hop into it and start the engine. Now, this is what you call exposure. The thrill is in the possibility of being caught. I lay down and spread my legs open, his eyes widen at the prospect of what is to come. I bite my lip and gesture with my finger for him to get in between my thighs. He takes his jogging bottoms off completely this time and his throbbing penis greets me again. I know he wants to stick it in me but I stop him because I have the urge to see what it tastes like. He clocks onto this pretty quickly and gives me the access I require.

I stare up at him whilst I suck and swirl my tongue playfully. This eye contact is getting him even more hot under the collar, so the party in my mouth comes to a quick end as he grabs my legs and pulls them towards him. He rolls my dress up above my hips and sticks the tip in, teasing me obviously. This guy knows what he's doing but I want to take the reins on this one, so I swivel my hips and thrust my body on top of his. I land on his dick with ease as I am already soaking wet and start riding him. I can tell he likes to keep the control in the bedroom but I do this for a living and of course he is giving in to my strategic wiles.

He is reaching his limit as I pick up the pace in a circular motion. Four, three, two, one, he's done. I ease myself off and sit down opposite him. He smiles and reaches into a rucksack he has left in the corner of the boat. Out comes the fat envelope with my well-earned money in. He passes it to me and gives me a wink before steering the boat back to land. Time to get on home and have a long relaxing bath, I think.

Chapter Nine

Sunday fun-day has arrived, or as I like to call it "pretend to be normal for the benefit of lasting friendship" day. Time to meet the gang for a brunch of some kind and consume at least half a bottle of wine betwixt the three of us (mainly me). I do enjoy exchanging pleasantries with dear old Jack and Stacy. I wonder what is on the agenda for today's topic of conversation. Has Jack been fighting with his boyfriend again? Did Stacy forget to do the weekly shop again? The possibilities are endless. This type of mundane talk is exactly what I need to distract myself from my other life. I could not be happier discussing this pointless shit with my two best friends.

We decide to go to the Bluebird in Chelsea, this is a wonderful place to meet clients but I must resist…I opt for an eggs benedict with a latte because this is my favourite thing to eat for breakfast when the opportunity arises.

As I gently stab at my eggs, Stacy formulates a conversation with me about work. "So, Cami, how is work? Is that knobhead Bobby still trying to get into your pants every five minutes?" I laugh at her choice of the word knobhead, this does fit him perfectly.

"Ha-ha! Of course, Stacy, lunch is still awkward as fuck. He has yet to accomplish the hint taking abilities of a normal functioning human." This comment causes Jack to involuntarily spit his mouthful of coffee all over the table and all three of us burst into laughter.

We move on from the coffee to the wine (thank god) and then me and Stacy sit back and listen to Jack's sex stories. Him and Tom really do have some of the strangest tales to tell especially when they've had a drink, the events that usually follow are always entertaining to listen to.

My date with Mr twat face James is coming up this week. He wants to meet for coffee on my lunch break on Wednesday. Somehow, I find it ironic that 'hump day' is the day he chooses, he could have chosen Tuesday or even Thursday but oh no, that is not the case. Wow, I really am reading way too much into things there aren't I. Stop being a class A weirdo girl! Someone punch me in the uterus because I am becoming a right pussy.

It's Tuesday morning and I am daydreaming about what kind of cock James has. The shape is very important, too thin and it's pointless having sex and too thick, I'd have to lube it up to the max to make it a bit easier for my vagina. Both are equally disappointing so I am hoping for a bang in the middle kind of penis. God, I am so horny right now, I cannot believe that in the dating world it is frowned upon to have sex on the first date. I think you should be able to do whatever you like as long as you are cautious. You get those girls that pretend that it's beneath them or something ridiculous however, these girls are l-y-i-n-g to avoid being judged by the cruel society we live in these days.

Annoying Bobby tries to interact with me yet again at lunch time but he can tell I am distracted. I can't even eat my chicken and bacon sandwich without feeling sick which is an indication that I am nervous about tomorrow. How does one even act on a date? It's been so long I have lost all recollection of dating do's and don'ts. Silly isn't it; I can fuck a man no problem but when I start catching feelings I'm hopeless. Feelings make you say and do things that you wouldn't dream of and this truly, truly has rendered me retarded.

"Bobby, have you ever been in love?"

"Well, erm, sure I have. It's a tough burden to bear though I must admit. You must be in it to win it, Cammy. Why, is there a special someone in your life worth mentioning aye?"

"No Bobby, it isn't you sweetie. Ha-ha, well there could be potential somewhere down the line but I am not so sure. His name is James." Name dropping is always a good start however this man has been trying to get into my pants since the day I started working at the office, so I don't think any of my ploys to diminish his interest are ever going to work unless I quit my job. Food for thought there…

I get home still feeling sick with nerves. I wish they would just fuck off. Although, this means I don't have to prepare dinner for the evening if one is looking at the situation from a positive perspective. I kick off my shoes and hunt down my tracksuit bottoms and a comfy vest to change into. I have been feeling so irritable this week, I wonder if it is my time of the month and think…shit! I have been so caught up in my master plan that I haven't even been paying attention. Since this realisation, my body has decided to wake up smell the roses because ouch, I start cramping up.

You know, feeling like your ovaries are being stabbed is one thing but having to bleed as well really makes periods a girl's worst enemy. I pull myself up off the sofa and dive towards the 'period supply drawer'. I have to prepare myself for 'if' I decide to bleed any time soon. Well, at least now I know for sure I won't be tempted to take James home tomorrow, yay.

As expected, my mood was that of a tyrant all morning at work. I honestly cannot thank mother nature enough for bestowing this dreaded curse on women. I know I am no fun to be around at this present state and this makes me worry for my date. I just hope to god that James is mature enough to see past my banshee ways for the entirety of our lunching and still want to take me out a second time. Let's see, should I bet on those odds?

It is quarter to twelve on the clock, fifteen minutes to go, just ticking away. I excuse myself to the bathroom so that I can freshen up a bit. He texted me to confirm the coffee place and time as I wait for the remaining five minutes.

We opted for a coffee shop called Notes. Their coffee is divine if I do say so, myself and so I am more than okay with the choice made. I get there and he is sitting outside smoking a cigarette. He looks up when he sees me, giving me, yes you guessed it, a cheeky wink. Gosh, he seems so predictable but I love it. I prance over to the chairs and take the seat opposite him.

"Well, you're a sight for sore eyes aren't you, babe!" I try to withhold the blushing I find myself experiencing but fail miserably. Shit.

"Hello to you, too Mr!"

"Shall we go inside or do you mind ordering out here? The weather isn't too shabby today but it's up to you."

I reply, "Let's stay out here and enjoy the weather as it is likely to be shite tomorrow living in London as I am sure you are well aware." He chuckles knowingly and then we order the drinks. I am craving a muffin so I order one of those as well.

"So, Camilla, tell me about yourself? I keep miraculously bumping into you without knowing much else apart from the fact you're a little fitty with a smart mouth. As appealing as both of those attributes may be, darl, I am intrigued to know a bit more."

Well, this guy doesn't beat around the bush does he, went straight in for the compliment. His confidence is definitely also very appealing. Obviously, I will have to reiterate the question he just asked me because he clearly doesn't know I went all FBI on his ass. "Well, firstly, thank you for the compliment. Secondly, gosh, there isn't much going on in my life that is of much interest. I live quite the normal life."

"I may intrigue you but that's just because I am highly charming! Now, tell me about yourself because I am 90% sure, you are more interesting than I am!" That's it, Cam, change the subject, good girl.

However, rather than immediately showering me with his many attributes, he decides to reach out his hand and start caressing my forearm. Brilliant. This kind of contact was not expected on the hormonal journey nature has succumbed me to. Fuck me. I feel like I just want to grab his hand and stick it in my knickers but that would just be a bloody mess, now wouldn't it? (literally)So, I opt with the 'just let him do his thing' scenario.

You know God is a right bastard, causing women to have periods is enough torture any given week, but to make our sex drive increase with it is just cruelty. I get that there are other holes to be used in these situations (which luckily I have no issue with) but not all girls are like me and do not allow a man anywhere near their arsehole or their mouth. Happy endings for no one. Ah, now he wants to answer my question, finally.

"Well to be honest with you, Cam, I would much rather listen to you talk all day than bore you with my details. I will not be rude though and so I'll tell you a little something that not a lot of people know." Wait for it…he's going to drop the undercover police officer shit on me any minute now!

"So, here goes, it's a funny story really! I was holidaying in Cancun and met this girl. We were both plastered and ended up in a tattoo shop. Next thing you know, I wake up on the beach and find myself branded with this chicks name on my arse cheek…It is probably the most embarrassing thing ever, especially since I don't even remember what she looks like but I thought I should pre-warn you in case I accidently drop my pants in front of you. Don't worry though, this would only occur if I were intoxicated to an excessive amount and I have not pre-empted anything." He chuckles to himself at this because he knows he is full of shit.

Right, so aside from picturing his perfectly shaped bottom, I feel like that was a bit of an anti-climax. Although, I am finding myself incredibly jealous and hoping it isn't a stupid name like Mary as this name does not deserve to even be in the vicinity. Wow, okay, I sound like a psychopath. He obviously doesn't feel that we're on that level yet to start discussing his secret FBI life but I really wanted him to tell me so I can make sure that he doesn't find out I am an escort.

Oh, Bollocks to that, who am I kidding? I'll be on his bloody hitlist indefinitely I know it. I should probably run away whilst I still have the chance. I guess prison won't be so bad, I can get myself a bitch and everything…No, I cannot do this.

I have to respond to what he has told me now in a manner that I am not entirely comfortable with because I still fancy the shit out of him (even though this little confession made me feel a certain amount of rage) but if he isn't going to tell me his inspector gadget story, then I have to try and put him off me somehow so I don't have to move away or resort to plastic surgery and changing my name.

"Oh, that is really interesting, James and I would love to hear more but I have to go now, got lots of work to do." Before he has a chance to respond, I get up, chuck a fiver in his direction like he's a cheap stripper and start speed walking. Shit, shit, shit, shit, shit! Only I would end up liking a guy who I can't be with. The fairy-tale of Camilla and James has had to die and I am gutted. Won't let it bring me down though, plenty more fish in the sea who I can hide my double life from and do not own a gun.

Further to this, I gather that my impulsive actions probably haven't helped me in the slightest and I now look like a crazy bitch, however, better a crazy bitch then a dead one…

Since I left James at the coffee shop and returned to work, I have received but one message from him asking me if he did something wrong that I have kindly ignored. I do hope he doesn't end up calling me because ignoring that one message has been hard enough. Whilst I'm contemplating my life choices annoying bobby decides to swan over. God I do not have time for this today.

"Hey! Why the long face, Sugar?" Drop me out, Bobby! It's one thing to approach a lady whilst her uterus is falling apart but coming at me with that stupid comment may just get you a one-way ticket to the grave. Strong words you may say, but if you are a girl you will understand that this is the consequence.

"Hi, Bobby, what do I owe this pleasure?" Full on sarcasm there you mo-fo, please leave me alone.

"I was wondering if you would like to go for a drink after work, look like you need it!" Yep, still a clueless bonehead but he's got a point, I do need it even if it is with him. Christ, I hope he doesn't think this is the start of something.

We end up going to this little bar called all-bar-one which has some of the best cocktails in London. I am on my third sex-on-the-beach and due to not eating much today I am feeling the effects already. This is probably the worst idea I've had for a while but I feel like moping and need some male attention to cheer me up about James.

In my hazy state, I look at Bobby and think to myself if only he wasn't such a prat. He has such a pretty face. By this point, he is wasted and attempting to come on to me as usual. I thank my lucky stars that I am on my period because if me and Bobby were to fuck tonight, I would have to leave the country beyond any doubt. Nonetheless, I allow him to shower me with compliments and try and be his wing lady.

The least I can do is get some other poor girl to sleep with him or at least give him a hand-job. I scan the room and locate a hottie to my right. She is petite and brunette, perfect. I stroll over to her and introduce myself. "Hey there, my name is Camilla. I noticed you from across the room and you are gorgeous! Don't worry, I am not coming over here to chat you up, it's my friend over there, he is into you and seeing as you are here alone I assume you are looking to meet someone. What do you reckon? Would you fuck him or at least offer him a pleasant hand-job?" I gesture over to Bobby who is oblivious to what is going on right now. The little hottie looks pensive, this is a good thing. It means she is considering her options. I like this girl, maybe we could exchange digits and be buddies.

"You know what, he is good looking and I am looking for some fun. Sure, why not. Introduce me, will you? My name is Paige." Sweet! This girl is a woman who knows what she wants.

We walk over to Bobby and I introduce the two of them. Bobby's eyes light up and she bites her lip whilst whispering what I can only imagine is absolute filth in his ear. My work here is done so I bid them both a due and scurry off to get a cab. Whilst I am on my way home, I receive a text from Madam. I explain to her that I am on my cycle but should be done by the following Monday, which is perfect timing for the next client she has for me. Looks like I need to book last minute holiday because this shit is international. I am wanted in Dubai!

Chapter Ten

So, believe it or not, this is the first time I have been called to Dubai for work. I am not sure what I am letting myself in for which equally excites me and scares me a little bit…but in a curious way. I touchdown at the airport and I am super thirsty; it is hot up in here right now! Cannot wait to enjoy some sunshine whilst I'm here and maybe engage in some skinny dipping. I walk through customs finally after an extensive check and see my name being held up on a card; this must be my ride. I follow my driver outside and am not complaining when there is a nice Bentley waiting for me, the job has its perks!

I don't try and engage in small talk with him as he seems like he is paid to be serious. I actually don't know where he is taking me but I assume we are arriving at our destination soon. It is getting slightly dark out when he finally stops at what looks like a hotel but from the signage, it appears to be a club as well. Oh, I like this.

He opens the door for me and I make my way to the entrance. There is a reception desk as I walk in and sitting there waiting for me is a skinny blonde lady. She asks me to sign my name on the register and then leads me through a curtain and into the club.

The whole place is dark with spots of light by a series of doors. Where the hell is everyone? I try not to think about this too much and then we stop at one of the doors, the colour of this one was gold. I wonder if it is real gold or just coated gold? What? You can't blame me for asking myself this as I am in Dubai. She asks me to turn the handle and let myself in, what I am faced with ladies and gentlemen is a fucking orgy. I don't know where to look first, but I do notice one thing, everyone is partaking in anal sex. Is this the anal only room? As you have probably guessed, I'm game for anything, so I can totally roll with this. As I make my way around the room, I am intrigued with what I see. I am so tempted to get involved and just want to reach out and touch these beautiful people.

Apparently, though I am not allowed to get involved based on the look the security guard just gave me. He gestured for me to leave the room and enter the door on the other side of the room. I kindly oblige although I am slightly disappointed.

I walk through the door and there is a gentleman waiting for me with a couple women by his side in lingerie and in the left-hand corner is a pole. I think I know where this is heading. "Miss Camilla, thank you so much for coming down here to my club, I am so glad you accepted my request. Now, I am sure you liked what you saw in the previous room, however, taking part in this is something that is earnt. These two lovely ladies will help you get ready in the next room. I look forward to your performance."

Hell, yes! I get to pole dance! This is something I have always wanted to do and now I have the opportunity. I am taken into the next room and I am just surrounded by expensive lingerie. I scan the room for my options and a red lacey set catches my eye. I have to say that in my opinion, there is nothing sexier. I pick it up and get undressed. I then pick out a pair of black stockings to finish the look. Once I have this on, I am given a pair of shoes and then the two girls sit me down to do my hair and make-up. This is it, go time!

I stroll out of the room and the spotlight is on the pole, the rest of the room is pitch black. My heart is racing. I step into the spotlight and grab hold of the shimmering pole in front of me. I jump on to this, slowly swirling my body round and round its surface. I pull some sexy poses as I rub up against it and gyrate to the music.

I can't see my audience at all, but this just adds to the appeal. I am so turned on right now I can feel myself getting wetter and wetter. I slip a finger inside to get a closer look and it's no surprise I am dripping. I pull out and raise my finger to my mouth and suck, I love the taste of my own pussy. This is why I am an escort people, plain and simple.

I feel like I've put on enough of a show for now and hope I can fuck someone soon. I get off the podium and await my next instruction. There are a few moments silence and the anticipation is killing me. All of a sudden, I hear the voice again; "That was quite a performance, Camilla, especially the ending. You have earned yourself a place in our sex show, the one you walked through to get here is the main event. I assume you are quite clear on what you'll be engaging in, so I do not need to remind you. I'll be watching. Enjoy."

It's a good thing I love anal.

I walk back into the room, it's so hot and steamy in here and the stench of sex is overwhelming. It seems like they have all been at it for hours! I spy a tall, dark, handsome gentleman to my left with beautiful green eyes. He's eyeing up my body from head to toe and there is nothing subtle about it. I need to let him fuck me. He struts over to me, never losing eye contact. When we meet, he wastes no time as he bends me over the chaise lounge to my right and pulls my knickers to the side. He then spits on his hand and moistens up the area. I feel his cock edging its way inside, slowly teasing me and this makes me gasp. Once he has entered at full capacity, he pounds at me forcefully. I would scream his name if I knew it because it felt so good.

Chapter Eleven

So, you know, you hear stories of them people that just up and leave their job, their friends and their family and move to another country…that's what I did three months ago.

You can probably guess; I fell madly in love with that tall dark stranger I met in the sex club and you'd be right. Though, his name, my darlings, is Corey Jackson. I know previously I thought I was in love with that James but this was clearly not the case because I haven't felt emotion like this in my entire life. I am utterly besotted. I mean you don't just up and leave your entire life for a quick fling, this was the real deal.

Corey was not a fellow escort like me, he was actually a rich businessman out here in Dubai who took part in these sex parties for fun, until he met me of course. He has so much money that I don't even need to work. Plus, he actually doesn't want me to sleep with anyone else now, so that means that my escort days are over. Wow, over. It still feels so strange saying it.

I changed my phone number about a week ago because I could not deal with the constant calls and messages from my parents and my friends. I feel like such a selfish bitch however there comes a time in life where you have to be selfish and my time is now. Also, they don't know about my secret life, so to explain to them the reason why I am here would be tremendously awkward. To let them think I have gone off the radar because I am having a mental breakdown is best I think. Sorry, guys. I still love you.

So, life out here in Dubai is spectacular. It is hot every day which is so refreshing, I don't think I could ever get used to the shitty English weather again. It would probably send me into a deep depression forever and you can't put a price on happiness guys! Another benefit is that gorgeous glow I am currently sporting which makes me even more desirable. I love having a tan. My back garden is basically a beach and my new home is an actual mansion. Could life get any better?

Oh, and if any of you are concerned about Bubbles, don't worry, she's next to me right now. That little fucker is part of me and I could never let her go. She has also managed to score herself a boyfriend the flirt. Next door cat is on her case daily. They even have romantic diner dates where they catch mice and eat them together under the moonlight. It's really quite something.

Domestic life has become my new ideal. I just wanna bake cakes and shit all Sunday morning. So far, I have baked brownies, cheesecake, Victoria sponge and even attempted to make my own macaroons. Truth be told, on my first attempt, I did manage to give the entire staff food poisoning, but they all made it so positivity all around! I have since improved and now I am a cracking Betty Crocker.

Oh, how things have changed. I do sometimes wonder what state my parents are in following my spontaneous departure from their lives. Maybe I'll send them a cake as goodwill.

It's Saturday and I am just waking up. God last night was fun. I was literally having sex until the early hours of the morning with my delightful dream man Corey. His stamina is unbelievable; I just cannot get enough. If he doesn't put a ring on it soon, I will just lock him up so he can never leave me. To be fair, this is actually how we spend most of our evenings, so I am always waking up at midday or later. This however is not the case for my love, he goes to work every bloody day with zero hours sleep. I would worry about his wellbeing if he weren't fucking me so good.

I practically roll out of bed and find some roses on the dressing table. Ah, an abundance of white and red roses with a little note addressed to moi. He does this for me every Saturday...I mean come on, who doesn't love that kind of gesture? He doesn't miss a trick which sometimes makes me wonder if he is too good to be true. Most people would suggest this is the case however I do not associate myself with pessimists like this.

I run myself a bath and whack the cinnamon candles on. This bath lasts a good half an hour and by the time I am done my skin is shrivelled up like a prune. Time to bake some shit and then go for a jog on the beach. I'm used to the heat now thank god. Wasn't the case for the first couple of weeks I'll tell you that. Tried jogging on the beach and passed out. This was no joke. I was not prepared nor was I hydrated... probably shouldn't have had all that champagne beforehand.

Despite me being happy for my dear Bubbles finding love the same time I have; I hardly see the little bitch anymore. She is a whole new kind of pet, the outdoor kind. I miss my stay indoors cat to be honest. How dare she leave me on my own, she is supposed to be with me always. I don't think people buy pets just to let them roam the streets at all kinds of hours with their significant other! This is not what our relationship is about so she needs to think about her actions and reflect. That would be a great birthday present.

How have I managed to reach twenty-six and met the love of my life? My mum got married at this age, must be a sign. Time to start looking at wedding venues. Oh shit, am I for real right now? I never ever thought about this stuff ever. I have even thought about how many kids we are going to have and how beautiful they're going to be. I want at least three. Two girls and one boy. There was a time (three months ago) where all of this would seem so absurd to me. Now, it's the norm…like I can't go a day without thinking about it.

Ouch! I just broke a nail. God that shit hurts. Here I am just enjoying a nice sunbathe when 'ping' goes my phone. Oh, sweet Jesus, it's Madam! I never thought I'd see the day where she wasn't pimping me out and I suddenly felt pained at her message. How the fuck did she get this number? She definitely just went all PI on me and I can't hide my unmistakable glee that she went to all this effort to find me. Having said that, I haven't read the message yet, so it could be a bad thing. This thought automatically alters my mood and I am now feeling a small shred of anxiety appear. I was just about to turn on my front to let my equal tanning commence but I'm too nervous and that my friends is bollocks, quite frankly.

I hover my finger over the message for a further two minutes and then decide that if I wait any longer I'll faint from the stress. I open it and see a photo. A photo of Madam in Dubai, on the beach with a porn star martini with the message "I found you, my dear," written at the bottom.

The realisation that she is in Dubai and has been stalking me finally hits and I need a shot…or two. I don't even know how to reply and whilst I'm considering my options, 'ping' goes my phone again. "Join me for a porn star, lovey, I'll send you my location."

I spot her in the crowded beach and make my way over. She looks up and jumps out of her chair embracing me with a warm hug. I can't deny that it's nice to see a friendly face. I don't think I mentioned her first name earlier on, she likes to be addressed as Madam Featherley from a professional point of view. However, her first name is Barbara.

"Barbara! You better explain yourself!"

"Ha-ha, my love, *where there is a will there is a way*. I wasn't made aware of your abrupt departure from London as well as everyone else you know, so you can imagine my concern when I send you to a job in Dubai and you do not return! Now, you know I don't like to raise my voice or cause a scene however, I am truly disappointed that you upped and left the way you did. The clients have been asking about you for weeks now. They are going out of their minds. I need to meet this gentleman that has swept you off your feet like this! He must be pretty extraordinary to have managed to tame you. One of my best employees you are."

"Is it that obvious? Fuck…I can't even understand it myself to be honest. It's the craziest thing I have ever done and you know the types of things I have got up to in the escort business. It just feels right and I just took that risk. Is this all you came here for though Barbara or is there something else going on?"

She looked at me and said with a smile "Unless you are coming back to work, I am just here for the cocktails now!"

Barbara and I spent the next 48 hours drinking cocktails, sunbathing and dancing in bars until the sun came up. I urged her to stay longer; however, she said she couldn't leave the fellow escorts unsupervised for too long, so I said my goodbyes, feeling slightly emotional. That is the first friendly face I have seen in over three months.

On another note, it's that time where I can safely say I want to take the next step in settling down, the contraception is out of the window as of today! I never, ever pictured myself being at this stage in my life. Of course I always wanted kids, but having no man in my life and my previously chosen profession kind of put a spanner in the works…

So, that being said, I am now in the process of intentionally impregnating myself with my soulmate. Just so you don't think I'm some sort of psycho, he is fully aware of this and it was a mutual decision. I'm not going to trap the poor sod! Though, the thought of this does make me chuckle.

I love to imagine how beautiful our kids are going to be. They are going to be something else, definitely 10/10s and that isn't even me being arrogant it's just the sad truth. Sad for everyone else I mean. Probably should let my parents know I'm having kids now; they would be thrilled to know that their not-dead daughter is starting a family and that they can be grandparents. I can't decide if I should FaceTime them or give them a call. The pussy in me thinks a call would be safer but if I FaceTime them, it will be like they're here with me. Shit. What have I done? Why would I do this to my parents and friends? I have been pretty selfish to say the least and I need to buck my ideas up!

Maybe I should invite them to stay out here for a mini holiday. I'm sure they haven't had one in about 30 years. But oh god, thinking about all of the questions I'm going to get just hurts my head. I have royally fucked this situation up, haven't I?

How does one even approach a conversation with the sad excuse of a woman that is me? "Hey, Mum and Dad, I'm not dead, surprise!" Jesus, that was a bad start. I need to think about this a bit better. "Mum, Dad, I am so sorry that I upped and left without saying goodbye and moved to Dubai. There's just this guy here that I became horrifically obsessed with. Oh, and we're having babies." Hell, no. I will not let my parents in on my unhealthy obsession like that. And why would I use the word horrifically? That just makes me sound like I should be in a straight-jacket, so I don't end up smothering him to death.

I realise I am constantly contradicting myself when I say I'm not a psycho but continue to say psychopathic things, but I reckon we should just let that one slide because everyone is a psycho sometimes and I'm having my fair ride at it! So, back to the critical phone call to my parents…

I will just have to man up and do it, what is the worst that could happen? I hope they still have the same number. I find a good spot in the beach garden, down a glass of wine and hit FaceTime dial. It's ringing for quite some time and I almost decide to cut the call off but then pops up the bewildered faces of my parents. Should have probably text them to say new number first but it's too late now they can see it's me. "Mum, Dad, hey!" was all I could muster.

"Camilla, were you trying to give us a heart attack? You up and leave with no word. Me and your dad thought you were abducted! How dare you abandon us like this, you have some serious explaining to do, young lady!" Well, that wasn't as bad as I initially thought although assuming I've been abducted is a tad strong. I wonder if claiming insanity will save me having to explain myself. No, let's not be silly Cam.

"I do realise my departure was a little abrupt..." My mother decides to interrupt me mid-sentence.

"Damn straight it was! Did you ever consider our feelings? Your father sent out a search party and everything, you have been on the missing persons list for over three months!" Shit, shit, shit. My face has been plastered all over London, I did not think this through at all. Bollocks.

I hesitate, then reply with, "I'm really, really sorry, mum. I decided to take a mini holiday here in Dubai and then ended up meeting the love of my life so my thought process went out of the window and I lost all logical sense. I'm fine though so you don't need to worry anymore. In fact, why don't you and Dad visit? I'm sure you could do with some sun!" There was a painful silence for a couple of minutes which felt like hours. Can they say something, anything? Bit rude to ignore a holiday invite, it can't be that traumatising surely. I then try to picture myself being in their position and realise that of course it was fucking traumatising, so if anything, they are entitled to throttle me once they get here (if they get here) and I am a bad person.

"Camilla, we are severely disappointed in your actions and we will never forget what you have put us through! However, if you have finally got a boyfriend that's lasted more than five minutes, then we have to meet him! Dubai sounds fantastic. I assume you are paying for our flight as an apology so please book us on the next available flight this coming Friday and it better be first class! Look forward to seeing you, darling!" Ah, my parents.

I get them to email over their passport information and book them on the next available flight this coming Friday as so gracefully requested by my dear mother. Well this is exciting! My folks will get to meet the love of my life and I'm pretty sure my mum will fall in love with him too. My beautiful Corey. He really is something else.

It's Tuesday afternoon and I have asked Corey if I can meet him for lunch. We've been together three months now and boy has it flown by. It's about time he met my parents, and this was the perfect opportunity. We arranged to go to our favourite bar on the beach called Beach Bar & Grill. I arrive at 12:00 pm and he is already sitting there waiting for me with a glass of wine. "Hello, my love. You look beautiful, please sit." He's such a charmer. Every day he tells me I look beautiful and I will never get bored of hearing it.

"Hello, sweetie, thank you for the wine. I have some really exciting news to share with you!"

"Please, go on…"

"Well, you know how I haven't seen my parents in three months, I invited them out here to visit and to finally meet you! Their flight is already paid for, they'll be flying out this Friday. I cannot wait for you to meet them!"

"My darling! That is great news, I thought it was about time I met the people who brought you into the world. I cannot wait to meet them!" Could he be any more perfect?

"On that note, do you think you could extend your lunch for a little bit longer? Maybe to our little spot on the beach?" Yes, I was asking him for sex, it's only natural to want to fuck his brains out all the time! He laughed and cheekily grinned because he knows exactly what I meant.

"Of course, I thought you'd never ask." He grabbed my hand and led the way.

The day had arrived when my parents were visiting and I am actually so excited I can't breathe! Myself, Corey, Bubbles and Squeak (as I now call my cat and her boyfriend though his name is Sam), we're waiting at the airport, sign in hand. It has been a long time since I saw their faces and I know they are going to love it here. I just know they will love Corey too because it is impossible not to fall head over heels for the guy. I tried my best to not fall in love with him right away but who was I kidding? That failed miserably. It took just two weeks for us to say those magic words and the rest is history. I do sometimes think to myself that the whole thing happened so fast but I am a true believer in 'just going with it'. Do what you feel is right at the time and if it's a mistake, deal with it and move on. That is my life's philosophy guys. Life is too short to overthink anything but do try and think a little bit so the mistake isn't catastrophic and ruins your life. Bit dramatic but hey.

I check the flight has landed and that they are in the batch of arrivals. I am now jumping up and down to see if I can catch their heads in the sea of people. Though, Corey is six feet and so I should really leave that to him. I did show him a photo of my parents so he should know who to look for. "Camilla, I see them, my love! Coming this way on our left."

I knew he would come through. "Oh my god! Yes, I can see them, wave the sign in that direction!" After a few more shakes of the sign they caught our eye and ran over. "Mum, Dad! I am so happy to see you!"

We help them carry their bags to the car and drive home. Seeing as my parents don't know how rich my boyfriend is, they will be in for a shock when they see the 'house' which is actually a fucking mansion. As predicted, my parents jumped out of the car and stood there with their mouths wide open. *I feel ya, Mum and Dad, I had the same reaction when I first came to Corey's humble abode.* From the look on my mother's face, she definitely fancies him. I am as smug as can be. I show them to their room and tell them to be ready in an hour for dinner. Corey and I are taking them to our favourite restaurant/bar which I mentioned earlier on. They will have a chance to have a drink and relax a bit.

The time on the clock is exactly 7:45pm. We are leaving at 8 but I have been ready since half 7. I think I am just a bit overexcited, so I calm myself down with a nice glass of wine whilst I wait for everyone else. I am even ready before Corey which should be surprising as far as stereotypes go but I just proved you lot wrong! God, I love it when that happens…

The cab beeps its horn outside and down scurried my parents and my other half. They look like they are bonding which is promising. I mean, I cannot see any reason for them to not like Corey however, parents will find any excuse. Knock 'em dead, babe, they got nothing on you, you are perfection. Okay, okay, no one is perfect I know but he is pretty close. We pull up and as usual my love gets out first and opens my door, such a gentleman. We get a table in the corner overlooking the seafront. It is so beautiful this time of night.

Back in London though…

Chapter Twelve

"Can I have another shot please?" You know when you have been travelling all day on a poxy train from your shitty university because your boyfriend of three years was cheating on you with the busty barmaid called Laura in the local pub on campus? Ergh, I now officially hate that name! I have now resorted to my fifth shot of the evening which may not seem like a lot to some people but it's a heck of a lot for a lightweight like myself. I down it and wave my hand at the bartender to order another and then the strangest thing happened, a young man put his hand on mine and said "Camilla, it's not like you to be drinking alone. Let me join you." I lock eyes with him, and my first thought is, hold on a minute...my name is Darcy, who the fuck are you? My second thought is, fuck me he's fit and I am newly single. A case of mistaken identity never hurt anyone, did it?

I smile and try my best to act like I know who he is and then say, "Shall we go somewhere a bit quieter then?" He takes my hand and we walk towards the lift, shit, he has a room at the hotel? I am fucking terrified right now. It is not like me at all to have one-night stands, so this would be a first for me. That being said, my ex had no problem shagging for fun, so I should see what the fuss is about. Get my own back if you like. I feel like I most definitely would not be taking this kind of risk sober so the shots have given me that Dutch courage alright. I will totally regret this in the morning I know it.

We get to the room and he grabs my face, kissing it passionately and pushes me against the wall. Oh my god, Jack never kissed me like this. I feel instantly wet with excitement. He then picks me up and chucks me on the bed. Rips open my blouse and hikes my skirt up around my waist. I am so caught up in the moment that I forget that I have no idea who this man is. To my relief, he pulls out a condom and puts it on. Pulling my pants to the side, he sticks his penis inside of me, slowly. I cannot stop myself from moaning. This is just so intense and I have never experienced anything like this before. He is pumping and pumping away at me and involuntarily I dig my nails into the soft skin of his back just as he comes. I cannot believe what I have just done. What makes it worse is that after he gets dressed, he hands me an envelope full of cash. Have I just been paid for sex? This really seems like I have been paid for sex. "Until next time, Cammy darling," he says as he leaves the room.

I peek into the envelope and I'm not even joking, there is at least a grand in there. I jump for joy and discreetly leave the hotel, I am sure the bloke I just shagged is in the bar somewhere but luckily for me, it's jampacked, so he isn't getting a glimpse of my getaway. I feel the air on my face as I contemplate what I have maybe gotten myself into, a pickle if you will. Oddly enough, I like a pickle in my McDonald's Big Mac, so this could be the answer to those dreaded university debt woes that us students have to endure and suffer until we die. To the point, I know but you won't argue with me because you know it's true.

I crash at my friend Callum's house for the night seeing as my home is in Leicester and this journey into London was a spur of the moment kind of thing. Whilst I am here, I ask if I can use his laptop to do some homework. This wasn't actually what I was going to do at all, I must find out who this Camilla girl is. My guess is that she is a prostitute or an escort, technically the same thing but escorts subsequently get paid more, so this is where I am heading. I type into Google 'escort services, London' and scan the websites to see if I can find the lady in question. I keep scrolling and then click on one of the links. Jesus Christ! I have only just found her and it's like looking in a mirror. You know they say that there is a doppelganger out there for everyone, well they weren't fucking kidding.

This is huge. I have just been mistaken for a high-class escort who could quite possibly also be mistaken as my twin sister. This is crazy shit. Where do I go from here? Do I accept it as a one off and in the morning make my way back to Leicester, cry myself to sleep every night knowing I have to see Mr penisface who cheated on me almost every day whilst he gets off with that tart or do I take this as a sign? A sign that this is meant to happen, and I should embrace the experience. I have a dwell on this for about 10 minutes and then think, fuck it. Let's do this!

Okay, decision made. Now, I have to figure out how I get her clients to meet me. Should I just pose as her and write to them? No, course I shouldn't. I need to remember that the clients come to me I don't chase them in this scenario. Following that, I cannot just call up her pimp can I?

Well…thinking about it though, if a client got us confused, maybe this will be the same situation. Nope, too risky. I am sure she will pick up something different about me that isn't on the real escort in question. The conclusion I come to is that I will just have to branch out myself.

Decision made, I take full advantage of my credit card and get as many expensive outfits and shoes as I possibly can. I have to look the part, don't I? I have to say, this has given me a new lease of life that I didn't think I had and fucking love it! Next stop, the salon. I get myself a full pampering session, waxing, manicure, pedicure and a blow-dry. Seeing as I don't have a permanent residence here that I can stay at, I have to book myself into a hotel. I only plan on doing this thing for a couple of weeks so I thank my lucky stars I have enough money to carry this little experiment out. Wait, who am I kidding? It's not a little experiment it's a bloody huge one and there is a chance I may not pull it off. However, I pull myself out of that negative place because fuck it, that's why.

I set myself up in a beautiful suite with a wonderful view of London, the Park Plaza Hotel overlooking the parliament. This is also a good place to meet tourists I figured, so therefore the likelihood of another client confusing me minimises slightly. I doll myself up and head down to the bar for my first scouting session if you like. Like I'm looking for new talent or something. I am kind of freaking out a bit, I was under the influence last time and I haven't even had a drink yet. I was reading up about escorts and it's never good to drink heavily on the job. You have to have full control of the situation.

Situation controlled; I spy a gentleman in a nice suit sitting by himself across the bar. I have to try and make eye contact first, to show my interest. He looks smart, well groomed. This should be promising. I order a drink, not to actually drink it but to give the impression that I am drinking alone too and that I could use the company. Yes! He catches my eye and I try my best to give a knowing look. I think he figures this out because he picks up his drink and walks over. Game on.

"Hi, my name is Perry. What's a beautiful lady like yourself doing alone?"

"Darcy, nice to meet you," I respond, politely ignoring his question because also from my research I found out that he is just saying this as code for 'I know you are an escort' and he's assessing my body language. "So, Darcy, you fancy taking this drink upstairs?"

"Certainly, thought you'd never ask." That flirty remark adds to the confirmation of my position, I think…

Perry is staying on the top floor, a penthouse. This tells me he has money. I chose well minus the bloody joke of a name though. Who calls their son Perry? Anyhow, let's not dwell on the bad, he is definitely a decent looking chap, a bit on the short side though now that we've been walking side by side. He isn't wearing a wedding ring either, which I know isn't the end of the world because married men do pay for this kind of thing unfortunately for their wives, but it means I haven't got to feel guilty. I don't think I want to start out with a married man, although, shit. I didn't even know if the guy I met in the bar was married either, I was so caught up. Can't change it now, Darc, stop worrying about things you cannot change.

Once we are inside, he offers me a glass of champagne. Don't get absolutely slaughtered but accept a glass of champagne if offered. I take the glass flute and position myself on the chair at the left of the bed. He takes his suit jacket off and loosens his tie. "What is it exactly you are after?" I get straight to it.

"Straight to the point I see, I like it. I am looking for a good time, no funny business, though I like feet. Don't worry, I am no toe sucker, I just like to appreciate them up close. Would you mind slowly removing your shoes first?" Ha-ha, my first 'client' has a foot fetish. This is definitely escort territory now.

I slowly slide my hand down my leg towards my feet, exposing my stockings. I stare him right in the eyes when I put my hand on the sole of my left shoe, ready to take it off. I follow suit with the right shoe and then start rubbing my feet just like when you take your shoes off after a night out and they sting like a motherfucker. He is watching me intently for about ten minutes and then I decide it's time to take it to the next stage. I walk over to the bed, undress myself and put my hand out as a gesture for him to come over. He kindly obliges, tie fully off now, shirt undone and belt unbuckled. His trousers are now removed as well as his boxer shorts. I then remove his shirt and we are good to go.

He requests that we do the 69'er because he loves to get a blowjob, whilst eating pussy with feet in his face. I haven't given many blowjobs in my time, so I hope getting creative will help me out a little bit, but no biting, remember the no biting rule is explicitly important. We get into position and I give it my best shot. Swirling my tongue as I suck. I have never swallowed cum before but I am sure that is what is going to happen. I wonder what it tastes like. I never did with my ex-boyfriend though he badgered me about it. I am a new woman now and swallowing is on the agenda. Surprisingly, I am enjoying this however if he takes any longer I am going to get lockjaw. What will make this end quicker? I don't really feel too pleased about what I am about to do but it's taking too long. I get another condom out from my bag and stick a finger up his bum. This should do the trick. Yes, thank god, out it comes into my mouth and down my throat. Yikes. Oh, and if you are wondering why I used a condom, this is standard practice for hygiene purposes.

I can 100% say I enjoyed the swallowing and wish I'd done it sooner. Actually, scratch that, my ex is a wanker, he didn't deserve it. I freshen up and he takes a shower. I wait for him to finish and he passes me a bunch of notes from his wallet. Ah, thanks, Perry, you shouldn't have. You know what, there is something about being paid for sex that makes all your inhibitions seem to disappear. You basically act like a professional the minute the process gets started, almost like you putting on an Oscar-winning performance. I consider heading back to the bar to pick up another punter but leave it for tonight and give myself a pat on the back for a successful evening. I'm not sure I'm at that level yet.

After having a long lie in, a sudden fear dawned on me. I haven't even got my uni work with me, what if I fall behind? Nonsense. I remember that I am ahead of the class and I am a fucking superstar so what's two weeks really? I can do that shit in my sleep. All perked up again I order room service. I am famished! I switch on my laptop and find myself checking to see if I have any reviews. Well, obviously, I don't have one from last night because the gentleman didn't think I was Camilla. However, the first man should have written a review surely. I open up Camilla's page and scan down to the comments page. Eek…random guy from the bar has left a review! First thing I see is the number of stars he has left, fuck me, I got 4.5 stars out of 5. This is unbelievable. His comment reads "never fails to disappoint. Was great to experience Camilla and her expertise again. Highly recommend." Hells, yeah! Oh, bugger, her madam (not pimp) reads these reviews doesn't she…

"Never fails to disappoint. Was great to experience Camilla and her expertise again. Highly recommend." This can't be right. Camilla is in Dubai with her future husband right now, this review is from a few days ago. What the actual fuck? Barbara looks at this review in bewilderment. I need to call this client to see if there has been some kind of mistake. "Hi, my darling, it's your favourite madam! I am just calling to ask if you are 100% sure you were with Camilla the other night as per your review?"

"Hello, well yes of course it was her. I know it was her. Why do you ask?"

"Oh, well you see I am just checking that the clientele are seeing the right people as per the diary but if she was with you then not to worry, I am glad the standard was still first class as always! Ta, darling." Hmmm, it would seem we have a little copycat on our hands here. Interesting.

With her new-found knowledge, Barbara thought to herself what to do next. Catch this copycat out or just embrace it? Camilla isn't coming back anytime soon and so this can bring some business back to the company. She decides to try and find out who this girl is and put her on the books as Camilla. Yeah, that is a great idea.

Oh, *ignorance is bliss*, isn't it when you have no idea that your plan has fucked up. Well, not entirely fucked up. I am none the wiser that Camilla's pimp/madam is on to me as I woke up in the Park Plaza with a stack of cash and a smile on my face just moments earlier. After checking this review on my expert shagging skills, I jump in the shower and get ready to go out for the day. I don't know if I am ready to be a daytime escort just yet so I will go out and enjoy the money I have worked for.

My family are middle-class citizens with a comfortable amount of money in their pockets, so shopping the highstreets' designers has been within my reach a couple of times for special occasions like my birthday. However, great a perk that is, I haven't experienced wealth of my own like this, out of my own pocket and I have to tell you it feels incredible. I scan the shelves for a nice new handbag, a couple pairs of shoes and a few new bits of clobber so I can look the part even more.

A tiresome three hours that shopping trip turned out to be. I think it's time to stop off into Starbucks and get a nice coffee and muffin. I decide to sit in, so I can get a bit of a rest, chill out a little bit and people watch. There is something so fascinating about watching people and their behaviours. How they walk, what their body language suggests etc. I have to be a bit tactful sometimes because you do get those people that think you're staring at them and they feel the need to get their back up about it. These kinds of people are what I like to call massive arseholes.

I am taking a nibble out of my muffin and then to my left I spy a smashing looking fella walking into Starbucks. He is dark and handsome, and I suspect—not English. I try not to make it obvious that I am checking him out but then out comes the words "Camilla? Is that you, mon Cherie?" Shit, he is one of her clients and he thinks I am her. Get into character, woman! Oh gosh, he is French. I love the French accent, it's beyond sexy. I wish I had a book in front of me that gave me a list of common French names, so I could attempt to reply like I know exactly what his name is. Sadly, I do not have one of those, so I just reply, "It's been a while, how are you, my darling?" Fuck, I hope she uses that word when she's talking to men. I try to hide my anxiety behind a smile. He returns the smile with a cheeky grin, thank god.

"Indeed, it has, I was quite torn up when you left me that night at the hotel back in France. Was not expecting my offer to be your only client to go that badly. I sincerely apologise for coming on too strong, Camilla. Truth is, I have missed our time together." Hold up...she turned him down? Was she fucking crazy? Oh no wait, I get it. He was probably crazy possessive. Now, I am definitely certain this was a bad coincidence. It's Karma. How do I get out of this one? I can't sleep with him even though I am so tempted to because she left for a reason, but what is my excuse going to be? Oh shit, I don't even know his name, let's hope his coffee is finished, so I can rely on the kind barista to give me his fucking name. "Grande latte for Claude." Thank you, Jim, thank you so much. I will definitely give you a tip.

"Claude, I am terribly sorry about how we left things; however, I am in a relationship now, so this wouldn't be able to rekindle. Thank you for coming over and chatting to me, it has been great catching up!"

"Ah, I should have guessed someone would snap you up at some point, I wanted to myself at one point. It's been a pleasure to meet your acquaintance again, mon Cherie, take care." And just like that, he walked out of the door. Can't help but think I must have dodged a bullet there. Once he is out of sight, I get up and tip Jim for his efforts.

I stroll back to the hotel but to my dismay, it starts to rain. I hate rain with a passion. Why would it just go ahead and ruin my day like this, so fucking selfish. I run for cover where I can and struggle to come to terms with the fact that I did not pack an umbrella. Shame on me for being so unbelievably pathetic. The rain finally stops after a solid thirty minutes. That is taking the piss if you ask me. I continue on route back to the hotel and jump in the shower. Without my knowledge, Barbara had been tracking my whereabouts and was actually waiting downstairs in the bar area.

I get out of the shower and the room service telephone rings, it's reception. "Miss Darcy, you have a guest waiting for you in the bar area."

"Oh, great thanks." Who the fuck is downstairs waiting for me? No one knows I am staying here; this is beyond freaky. I cannot contain my panic and oh behold, a panic attack comes on in full swing. OMG, OMG, OMG, this is so not good. I am struggling to breathe and so I run towards the windows to get them open, for fucks sake, they have a safety latch on them and only open a fraction. This is not going to have any effect whatsoever. I have to get outside. I grab the complimentary bath robe and slippers and my room key and head for the lift. My chest pains are intensifying now and I feel like I am going to die. I reach ground floor and can feel my heart pumping, not far now. I try act as normal as possible but am aware I look like I am having a panic attack, so what is the point I ask myself. Ahhhh, fresh air. I sit down on the steps outside and take deep breaths.

"You okay, m' love?" I look up and there is this stunningly elegant looking lady hovering over me. She has expensive clothes and looks very well put together. In my anxious state, I can tell she isn't a police officer so my next guess would be she is Camilla's madam. She sits down next to me and holds my hand, starts breathing with me and rubbing my back to help calm me down. I feel my chest loosen and my breathing getting back to normal. "That's it, my darling, very good now."

"Who are you?" I ask. The lady helps me get up off the wet steps and takes me inside.

"I'd be happy to discuss this in your suite as I can tell you aren't in a state to be in a public bar right now, sweetie." I just find myself nodding and taking her to my floor.

I sit down on the edge of the bed and she heads to the mini bar and pours me a drink. "This will help calm your nerves." I take it from her hand and take a sip. "So, I realise this may seem like a bit of a coincidence, however, don't be fooled. It is not. I tracked you down and found out this is where you were staying. I think you owe me an explanation as to why one of my girls is still getting reviews on the website when she is happily settled in Dubai with her new beau. Now, don't worry, I am not angry at all, darling, I am actually rather impressed with you and how you are the spitting image of my dear Camilla. Oh, sorry sweetie, my name is Barbara. I am the madam of a very successful independent escort agency."

Knew it. Told you, didn't I? I had an inkling it was her. Of course, she would have the resources to track me down so this was only just a matter of a time. "Hello, Barbara. I am very aware of what I've done here. It wasn't my initial intention, what happened was I jumped on a train to London to get away from my cheating boyfriend at uni and was mistaken for Camilla in a bar. I was so surprised how liberated I felt after that experience, so I kind of played a bit of a game here. I do hope you understand I am not looking to give your agency a bad reputation and I will stop this if you want me to. I am so sorry!"

"Nonsense, darling! I could use you for a little while longer if you want to carry on making money and enjoying yourself. What do you say? You in?"

What do you think my answer was? Why the fuck not.

Chapter Thirteen

So, as it happens, I am blissfully unaware of the identity thief business going on in London. Reason I say blissful is because I am still in absolute bliss with Corey. He makes me the happiest woman alive even though we fight like cat and dog sometimes. You know when you get two passionate people together, yes, the fights are intense but so is everyday life with them because you are both so passionate about each other. This is not for everyone because some people prefer a simple, easy type of relationship but I just don't see myself ever having one of those and I am not sure I would ever want to change what I have with my man. I am pre-warning you lot that I am feeling rather gushy and will continue to express my feelings towards this man I like to call home. If you are not the emotional type and will cringe at me then what I have to say to you is fuck off then, you heartless wankers.

Anyway, as I was saying, I can honestly say that I have never felt a love like this in all my life. I know I joke about being a lonely spinster whore and being fine with that, which is still technically true. However, I would trade it all again for my Corey. People may call me nuts but he is the happy ending I was supposed to have, I know it. Relationships are not meant to be perfect, two people in love is never something to take for granted. Ride or die and all that just like Jay Z and Beyoncé. God, I love that song they collaborated on, what was it...Bonnie and Clyde. Minus the murdering and robbery of course.

I can't quite see my life without him in it now either. If you asked me this when I first met him, yes, I was definitely infatuated with his beauty and skills in the bedroom however, I am so besotted with him that a life without him in it just doesn't sound right to me. Wow, I really am a woman obsessed. I do not care though; I will shout it from the rooftops loud enough for the entire world to hear and I am going to have his babies. Speaking of which, we are currently trying to make exactly that happen.

Since my parents had come to visit and had nothing but good things to say about him, this gave me the green light I was already gunning for anyway with or without their approval because I am an independent woman and make my own decisions. I am even starting to call it 'making love' rather than fucking or shagging which is also a huge deal to me. I always found it easier to be single and do the job that I do because there were no complications. The only feelings I did get were tingles in my vag and that was what I was used to. Okay, yes, I did have a thing for that James Splinter twat who gave me butterflies but the butterflies I feel now are almost constantly somersaulting in my stomach which I can admit is annoying but I embrace it now.

Back to the baby making. I have downloaded this app which tells you when you are ovulating and when you are most likely to get pregnant, so I am always on the ball. I really, really want to have his babies, so I am taking no chances, being very proactive. Obviously, I am not scheduling sex into the diary because routine life is not my kind of life at the best of times and I am not a robot. Robots are not sexy, so I am still keeping the excitement up.

Oh yeah! I almost forgot, my birthday is coming up soon, 9 March to be exact. I will be 27 years of age. I take a moment to reflect on this past year and what I have achieved. Managed to catch feelings twice, leave both my jobs, moved to Dubai and now, I am starting a family. Shit, that is a lot to take in. You know what I have also realised? If Corey and I ever did break up, it would only ever be him to do the leaving. As sad as it may sound, I could not mutter those words to him when I am so in love with him but if I had no other choice, I'd let him go. Omg, that went down a bit of a negative route didn't it. Best not dwell on the thought too much and remain positive like normal. Eugh, that was awful.

Like most of my birthdays, I am not usually one for extravagant parties etc. I don't see what the big deal is, why are you celebrating my age this much? I like to keep it small and intimate, just close friends and family. You are probably thinking that I seem like the type of girl to crave a big party, but you couldn't be more wrong. Remember, I mentioned before about layers and Shrek quotes? My escort self does love a party, but my normal self is quite relaxed. I made sure to let Corey know not to go overboard with my birthday plans and so just like a gem he reserves a table for a nice little dinner. It's a shame my mum and dad couldn't stay long enough to be here for my birthday but it's alright, I will just FaceTime them later.

I feel truly settled for the first time in my life and am not missing London one bit at present. Happy birthday to me!

Chapter Fourteen

It's 7:00 pm and I am going to a new client's house this evening. Madam (as I now call her) has sent me the address and some personal details about the client. Apparently, his name is Stan, he is a lawyer with a fetish for the good old golden shower. Yes, I said golden shower. Before you become an escort, these are the kinds of things you don't ever dream of doing but somehow being an escort creates a whole different identity and you feel like you can do almost everything you thought you wouldn't. it's an intoxicating feeling.

I pull up outside his place in Kensington, Chelsea. Yikes, his house is huge. I also would like to note how much I love wearing stockings now, they feel so good on my skin and make me feel so sexy. Isn't it amazing how certain clothes and accessories can make you feel any way you want them to? I slowly stroll up the pathway and knock on the door. To differentiate between who is knocking on his door, he asks that ladies like myself knock and everyone else rings the doorbell and knocks. He waits about five minutes to see if the bell rings and then when it doesn't, he knows what to expect. It's not rocket science for sure but hey, it works for him!

Out he comes wearing a very expensive suit, surely, he doesn't want me to urinate on that. Mind you, he's loaded so he probably has 100 others just like it. I wonder what type of lawyer he is. Apparently, I can't ask any questions or say one word until he says so. Bearing that in mind, I step into his hallway waiting for my instructions. He tells me to take off all of my clothes but to leave my stockings on. I follow him up the stairs and into the bedroom. There is a plastic sheet spread out on the floor, he lies down. Well, that was interesting.

When someone asks you what you do for a living and you say I pee on people for money, I wonder what kind of response you would actually get? Obviously, I am not about to tell my mum and dad what I am doing spending all this time in London but as you remember I am a student as well and though I am not in my uni halls currently, I still want to pass my degree. I don't think I mentioned what I was studying though so here goes. I am studying criminal psychology and to be honest I was hoping to work my way up to being a detective or something.

I sit in my hotel room studying away, feeling like a hypocrite but also feeling like I am getting real insight to the life of an escort. It will definitely add a bit of flare to my essays. I get a text from Madam; she says I have a client later on this evening. Apparently, he likes dressing up. This could be a fun night; I love a good costume!

I turn up at the address given to me, excited to play dress up and then when I enter, I see a bunch of baby toys. Wow, this is awkward, he has kids. I love kids as much as the next person but I now think he has a wife which isn't so ideal. I was told to let myself in, so I haven't actually seen the gentleman yet. I make my way up the stairs and see a door left slightly open. He must be in there. I open the door and what I see is a fully-grown man dressed as a baby. This has got to be one of the funniest things I have ever seen but I have to remain professional. This I am still learning because let's be honest, I haven't spent an awful amount of time practicing this trade, I kind of just fell into it. Desperate times call for desperate measures and all that jazz.

I have some young cousins that I babysit for sometimes so I shouldn't find this too hard. I put down my bag, remove my shoes and my coat. If I am going to be playing mum I have to be comfortable. I walk over to him and he starts clapping his hands saying "Mama, mama!" Aw, that's cute.

"Mummy is here, darling, now what do you want to do? Shall we play?" He nods his head frantically at this notion, so he's definitely in the playing mood, ironically. I will admit, this is making me a bit nervous but I have to prepare myself for these kinds of possibilities. I bet Camilla was a pro at this. She strikes me as a proper professional who lacks fear. You have to be pretty fearless to do this for a living. I look around the room at the selection of toys and pick a teddy bear that looks like it's been around for a while and pass it to him. He cuddles this with such a look of glee on his face. Step one complete, step two…

He soon grows bored of this teddy bear and pulls at my skirt. "Baby hungry, mama," he proclaims. I look around the room, there isn't any food in sight, so I have to go downstairs to the kitchen. You'll probably not be surprised by this, or you might be, I open his cupboards and his fridge and all that is there are jars of baby food. He has the largest selection I have ever seen. There is so much to choose from. I try and work out what his favourite must be and conclude he's rather fond of the spaghetti bolognaise and the creamy porridge so I grab both. Doesn't seem like the best combination but if he is taking this baby thing seriously it shouldn't matter.

I present the two jars and he grabs them out of my hand and starts pouring it down his mouth making a bloody mess! He then chucks them across the room and starts crying and screaming. Oh, Jesus what now? What can I do...I mustn't lose my patience, so I attempt to calm him down by taking him in my arms and rocking him, this seems to do the trick and he falls asleep? I ease him off of me and then search the room for my money because he is out for the count now. Ah, there it is.

Can tick this off my list of things I've never experienced now, which to be honest is ever-growing at this point in my life. But you know what hasn't happened whilst I have been in London. My scumbag cheating ex hasn't even attempted to contact me or track me down. What a disappointment. I mean, I don't want him back or anything, but it would be nice to think he was struggling without my presence. I mean come on, not even one drunken text. I know that barmaid had huge knockers, but we had a meaningful relationship at one point and to think I wasted years of my life with someone who doesn't appreciate me. Well, it's his loss.

It is hard to imagine how much my life has changed these past few weeks. I just treated a grown man as a giant baby and I didn't hate it, life is good. I'm seriously fucked up.

So, with the events of yesterday playing on my mind, I chuckle to myself as I enjoy a three cheese toastie and a large oat latte. I mean I guess I should be popping champagne bottles or something and eating caviar based on my now increased income, but I cannot draw too much attention to myself, that is the number one rule to escorting. I haven't been doing this long, but I know that for damn sure. Minding my own business, I take another bite out of my toastie and a string of cheese attaches to my chin, whilst I look for a napkin a warm hand taps me on the shoulder. I tense up and look at the face staring down at me. He looks nice but maybe he is a customer of Camilla's which I haven't come across yet. He had deep blue eyes and brown hair, around 5'9ish I would say.

I smile awkwardly and he returns that smile with a warm almost knowing smile.

"Hi there, do I know you?" seems like a simple way to start this awkward encounter. He lets out a small laugh and replies, "I am almost certain you know who I am, darling, did I not leave that much of a memorable impression on our last encounter? It's James, James Splinter, come on, Camilla you must remember me!" Oh shit, he knows Camilla. He doesn't strike me as a client of hers, his demeanour is cool and calm, his approach is friendly. How the fuck do I figure this one out. I am racking my brains right now, but I cannot ignore him for much longer, so I just go with open honesty, "Oh my goodness! Ha-ha, I am so sorry, but my name is not Camilla, I am a student, my name is Darcy. Do I look like someone you know called Camilla? Maybe she is my doppelganger?" He looks slightly taken aback by this revelation which I think must be a good sign. "Wow, you know what, Darcy, I am not going to lie you do look very similar, but I do apologise for the intrusion! I do feel a bit embarrassed, please forgive me! I know this is going to sound stupid, but would you happen to know where she is or is that just nuts?"

Aw, bless him he is obviously looking for her. Sadly, I don't think I can help him, she is nowhere near here that's for sure. "No, I'm terribly sorry, the only thing I know about her is that I now look like her but that is as far as my knowledge goes! I do hope you find her…"

"Darling, please do not worry it was very clearly a longshot! You take care and enjoy your toastie, looks like it's getting cold!" And on that note, he left the coffee shop. Not an expert but I am pretty sure something odd was going on there, I hope she isn't in trouble because then shit, I would also end up in trouble! Yikes, I think this escorting lifestyle is too dangerous for me. I am way out of my league here. Maybe it is time for me to throw in the towel.

Chapter Fifteen

So, guys, this is my memoir I am sharing with you and I promised myself that I would be completely honest and open minded about my life. Corey and I have been trying for a baby for some time now and have had no joy. Due to this I thought I would make myself an appointment at the doctors to have a check-up which then turned into a referral and now I am sitting here with my test results. I have been diagnosed with endometriosis, a somewhat debilitating condition where the endometrial tissue that forms in a woman's uterus forms in other areas such as the ovaries and fallopian tubes, which of course is not normal. This also comes jampacked with wonderful side effects that to be honest I didn't know I had since the contraception I have been on for most of my adult life and in my profession, decreases these side effects. If you don't have a period, you don't have the excruciating pain and the heavy flows and the difficulty getting pregnant.

Of course, sharing this news with my other half was not easy and to be honest, it has put me off trying to conceive until further notice. He wants to try other methods that can assist in my potential pregnancy, but I'm just so disheartened now that I don't want to discuss any of it. This is what I tend to do, push people away rather than deal with my feelings. It is a poor way to handle the situation I am aware, but I just cannot help it right now. Corey has been understanding and sweet, but I can sense his disappointment, nonetheless. I don't want to be a disappointment to my partner, that feels like shit. I think what I need is a bit of time to get my head around my new-found knowledge of my reproductive system.

I curl up on my bed under the duvet despite the temperature outside and snuggle my darling Bubbles. I see her as my first child, and she means an extraordinary amount to me. Yes, I am fully aware that all pet owners feel this way about their pets, but I am talking about myself here, so the rest of the world doesn't matter. You know what, I could just become one of those cat ladies or buy a couple of dogs who can replace my burning maternal desire for children. It's funny, people probably stereotype me as an independent woman, freeing her inhibitions and not needing a man to fill a void in my heart, but they couldn't be more wrong. Yes, I do have sex for money (well I used to) but that doesn't mean I don't want to settle down and have kids one day. It's such a cruel world we live in, people assume what kind of person you are based on what is on the surface. I would make a fucking great mother thank you! My children would be lucky to have me, I have a lot of maternal love to give and I shouldn't be stripped of that right! Damn it.

Interestingly, I never thought I would see Camilla again, not after she ran out on our date and acted very strangely but seeing her name come up on my investigation really turned things around! When I met Camilla, we met in the airport in France, she was definitely a looker, the type that lit up a room from a mile away. That's why I approached her, well that and the fact she had fallen on her arse. We had an instant connection and I'd be lying if I said I was disappointed when we went our separate ways. Of course, this was too good to be true, and maybe that's why she ran off? Did she look into me? Find out I was actually an undercover inspector specialising in prostitution and things of that sort? I am not one to judge people too harshly, so to be honest her other means for income are her own and she has the power to make that choice because it's her life. That being said, unfortunately, I have been assigned to look into her Madam's business and arrest anyone who is involved so that does put a spanner in the works. From our extensive research, it just so happens that she is currently in Dubai which is why I thought when I saw that lookalike that this would have been too easy. I haven't got sufficient proof that she is soliciting sex for money, the reviews on the Madam's website and her name is not enough, I have to actually catch her in the act. Although, let's face it, her being on an escorting website is a good start. Next stop, Dubai.

Touch down in Dubai and emotions are running high right now. I love my job; I get the bad guys! However, this is not one of those situations, Camilla is a smart, sweet, strong, vibrant woman, she is not a cold-blooded killer. If she were, it almost feels like the end result would be better. This woman does things to me, so I have to be on my guard. It's really quite sad that these are the circumstances we are going to be reunited by. Then again, all I am really doing here is travelling across the world to question a woman I once had strong feelings for, what's the worst that could happen? Apparently, she lives here with a gentleman who goes by the name Corey. Not sure how I feel about this but who am I kidding? She's been with this guy for a while, we only had a couple encounters and one of them was cut short when she bailed.

Now, I am in my hotel room wondering how the fuck I can approach this without seeming like I am just in the right place at the right time. Even I wouldn't buy that! Luckily, I have time to come up with a plan. Sleep on it, that will do the trick.

The next day, I really felt the Dubai heat hit me, woke up covered in sweat, brilliant. I get up, make myself a coffee and jump in the shower. When I was dressed, I decided to look up all the local hotspots where Camilla may be or may end up. I write down an extensive list and decide to hit the ground running. My plan was to convince her that I was here for a holiday because Dubai is highly recommended. That seems believable enough but she might not even remember me, let's see shall we?

I check the local bars and restaurants and even the beach for a good few hours. Still no sign of her. I continue to do this for the next four days and unfortunately to my disappointment she doesn't seem to be leaving the confines of her house. I mean, I could easily look up her address, I'm the police for Christ's sake, but I don't want to be snooping on her that way unless I have absolutely no choice in the matter. Also, I do enjoy a good chase, part of the fun right? I glance down at my phone contemplating where to look next on my list and the next thing I know I look up and I bloody see her! In the flesh, 500 yards away from me. I look her up and down, she is wearing blue denim shorts, a white vest top and flipflops. She looks lovely. The Dubai sun is clearly adding to her glow. No, wait, James, focus! She is grabbing an aperol spritz and sitting down overlooking the beach. I need to get my game face on before I walk up to her and stutter. See, this is what I am saying, I don't stutter, I don't get nervous and stuttering is not something I have ever struggled with in the past. Pull yourself together, you're on a serious case here.

Holy shit, I am a great actress. Does James think I haven't spotted him? He is only 500 yards away from me. I have to play it cool and not act suspiciously because you remember when I cut our last encounter short because I found out he was an undercover police investigator? Well, I am pretty fucking certain he is here to arrest me…well, attempt to anyway. He hasn't got any real proof of my past profession, even the Madam's website isn't good enough because that can easily be adapted just like Wikipedia. People edit those pages left right and centre, might give it a go myself one day. I haven't been an active escort for over a year now so my status should be cancelled. This is the last thing I need with all these pregnancy issues I am currently experiencing. Couldn't he just fuck off? I really don't want to have a stroke at 27 years of age.

I bet you, he thought I wouldn't remember him, but I do. His cheeky smile and blue eyes are hard to forget. Imagine where we might have been if things were different and I had a normal life. Well, that's what I have been trying to build here with Corey. He is so lovely, and I have loved living here. Looks like I should start writing my will though or do a runner. A runner seems the most likely option because it's easier to jump on a plane and leave your long-term partner than it is to write a list of what you are leaving behind once you depart this world. Where should I go? I could go to Italy or even America. No, to be honest, America may not be the best idea, too many states to choose from when you need a quick exit strategy. I gulp my aperol spritz as appose to sipping it but maybe I should slow down, cannot lose my cool. Oh god, he's strolling over. This could go very badly.

Right, I have made the conscious choice to walk over there now, I cannot waste any more time sitting here twiddling my thumbs. I wonder how this is going to go down...

"Hello, stranger, is this seat taken?" Good one, James.

"Oh my god, James? Is that you! What on earth are you doing here? The English weather not doing you any favours?" Good, strong response, Cam.

"Well, of course, you know what the weather is like, thought I'd have myself a little holiday! Are you here on holiday as well?" Keep it strong, fella, keep it strong.

"Well, funny you should ask, it's quite a funny story. I basically came here for a short holiday and then ended up meeting someone out here. His name is Corey, we live together, it was all a bit crazy to be honest but it's been a great experience. He is wonderful! Are you here by yourself or with some friends?"

"Ah, so you are off the market? Strange, I never pictured you to be living here with a house and all of that. He is a lucky guy. No, I am here by myself I am afraid." Jesus, I need to crack on with the prostitution interrogation, but I cannot bring myself to do it. Where do I even start? Looks like it's not happening today, I want to spend more time with her, so the interrogation is on hold.

"So, Cam, I would love a tour guide and seeing as you live here you would be the perfect volunteer if you should feel so obliged? Unless you have somewhere to be of course?" Here goes...

"Well, lucky for you, James, I have some free time. Corey is working, so I could do with the company. Let me finish my cocktail and I will be your guide, but you better pay attention, lots of skyscrapers to get through." How could I deny him a tour? He is on holiday…

Whilst I walk and talk doing my best tour guide impression, I cannot help but feel an urge to hold his hand, what the actual fuck. Stop, Camilla. What is it about old flames dropping back into your life with no warning? Further to this, I need to remember he is here to throw me in the slammer. He is not here by chance; I need to figure out a game plan.

We come to the end of our tour and I bid him goodnight. Corey should be back from work soon, so I rush back. When I get home, I open up my laptop and search Madam's site to see if it is still running or if it has been shut down already by James and his pack of wolves. To my surprise, it is still there. I scan the page for recent comments to see how business is going without me, I mean a girl got to know if she's being missed hasn't, she? I come across the most recent comments and there is one from last week, only it is a comment about me…what the fuck? Surely, this is a glitch or something because I haven't seen any clients out here in Dubai! The comment reads, "As per her reputation, Camilla did not disappoint. She is always a favourite, will always come back as a good time is expected." Martin.

Well, Martin, I do appreciate the compliment, but it was not me you shagged the other day. Oh my, someone is impersonating me back in London. What the fuck do I do about this? I fight the urge to call Madam, but I have no choice because she clearly knows it is not me and has allowed this to go on. The woman is definitely one to resume business as usual. I hear the front door open and up the stairs comes Corey. He knows I want some time to myself, so when he enters the bedroom, he slowly walks over and plants a sweet kiss on my forehead. "I hope you had a good day, honey."

I gaze up at him and nod my head, "It has been okay, took a nice long walk."

"Good to hear you went out and had some fresh air, I hope the walk helped you clear your mind with everything that has been going on lately. I love you and I am here for you." I cannot help but melt at these words because he is super sweet. I plant a warm kiss on his lips and give him a smile, so he knows I appreciate his support. With that, he turns around, turns the shower on and closes the bathroom door. Time to call Madam.

I am a bit nervous whilst I wait for her to pick up the phone. That sly devil better answer! On the fourth ring, I hear her voice, she sounds glad to hear from me…

"Hello, my darling!! What a pleasant surprise, do you miss me already?" Ha-ha, she is such a charmer, but I can see right through you Barbara!

"Hi there, Madam Barbara, of course, I miss you always, you know that! However, let's cut right to the chase here…I don't want to worry you or anything but a guy I was previously interested in turned out to be an undercover cop specialising in prostitution and all that malarkey and so was the reason I ran away to Dubai and never returned. Oh wait, it gets better. I was minding my business and out of the blue, he turns up in Dubai, seemingly knowing exactly where I would be. As lovely as it was to see him again, would you be able to shed some light on the situation please? Is he on to the girls?"

There is a long pause and I know she is deciding on whether she is going to spill all or try and deny knowledge for a bit longer. I am giving her a chance to come clean here! I hear her gulp and then she responds, "Okay, you got me, Cam. I don't enjoy lying to you I hope you know that but sometimes a girl has got to do what a girl got to do to keep a business afloat. Yes, I am aware of his investigation, in our line of work, Hun you have to have your wits about you. I can assure you; we are being very careful and have not given him any leads yet. That being said, I should probably come clean about something else too. It was very sad to see your remarkable skills leave the business. As you are fully aware you were one of our best girls, the clients loved you. Before I go on, you should know I had no idea this was going to happen…so a young lady who looks an awful lot like you was approached in a bar and ended up being paid for sex. She then realised she enjoyed this and so researched our business online. That is when she came across your profile and saw you were practically twins, I would imagine. So, she pretended to be you and then I found out because reviews were being left for you shortly after I returned back from visiting you in Dubai. I knew it was not you, so I tracked her down and asked her if she would like to carry on in your place…she happily agreed and so here we are. All cards on the table! I am so sorry, darling, but I didn't think it would matter until that cop started snooping. Are you mad? On a scale of 1–10, please do tell me?"

Wow, I didn't even need to press her she just let it all out! Shit, this is not good. What was she thinking! How mad am I? on a scale of 1–10? Fucking 100. I try to compose myself, but you know what it just doesn't happen. "How mad am I,

101

Barb? Ermmmmmm, pretty damn mad. How could you exploit me like that? And this doppelgänger, who is she do you even know what she does for a living or where she comes from? The poor girl is getting exploited too. You need to fire her, Madam, I am serious!"

"Alright, alright! Don't get your knickers in a twist, she already did leave. Obviously, she thought she was in over her head. The real problem we now face is how you are going to get that cop to leave you alone, he is obviously dedicated to the case seeing as he flew all the way out to Dubai to locate you. We need a plan, Cam, and we need one fast!"

I hate to admit it, but she is right. She may have exploited me and for that I will punish her, but we have more pressing matters. I know what I have to do, make James fall head over heels in love with me and convince him to stop his witch hunt. I haven't escorted in a long time now and to be honest I have been off the radar for long enough. However, that copycat has majorly put her foot in it because even though it hasn't physically been me, she has still been soliciting sex and either way they will try to track her down. I am going to need a bulletproof plan.

Chapter Sixteen

I don't want to sound like I am whipped or anything, but ever since Camilla gave me that tour, I cannot stop thinking about her. This was a bad idea. Did I really think I could hunt her down and charge her with soliciting sex like it was the easiest thing to do? I have come to a bit of a crossroads with my investigation. I have checked the website for the thriving business over and over and the most recent comments relating to Camilla just don't add up. She has been in Dubai for over a year now; there is substantial evidence to back this up with a clear paper trail of her coming here on holiday, meeting some rich bachelor and living with him to this date. Those comments cannot be related to her, they just cannot. Here poses my problem…wait, no, it cannot be? The girl from the coffee shop. I mistakenly confused her with Camilla, it was like they were twins. She couldn't be much older than 21, surely, she was a student or something. I put my detective hat on and consider the possibility that actually, this young girl was the one those comments were about and actually the clients also confused her with Camilla. What was her name again? Darcy, that was it. As painfully uncomfortable this may be, I have to investigate this Darcy chick. My sincerest apologies, sweetheart, but I'm just doing my job.

Okay, no this is not our culprit. The girl, Darcy, she is a university student. Clean record, nice family. I almost immediately cut her out of the investigation, there is no way she did this. Back to Camilla as prime suspect as much as I don't want to. Right, my plan now needs to be executed with brilliance. I know, I will make her fall madly in love with me (again) and then she will confess all. Need to make sure I keep my feelings to myself and lock them away if this plan is going to work. Lucky for me, I love a challenge!

Plan to seduce James is underway. Now, I know he is investigating me; he will be around for a while. Time to put on my sexiest clothes and charm him just like I did before, this will be no problem at all. One of my many talents I have acquired over the years is how to make men fall to your feet without much effort. I get out of bed, jump in the shower and make myself presentable. Bubbles is giving me a disapproving look from the corner of my eye, but I choose to ignore it. Would be a different story if she could speak so I am thankful at this time she is a cat with no words other than meow in her vocabulary. I am having some cramps in my tummy, stupid endometriosis ruining everything. I run over to the counter and pick up my painkillers prescribed by the doctor. As I was trying for kids with Corey, I have been gritting my teeth through the pain, but you know what, fuck it. I will go to the clinic now and request contraception. I know it was not part of the plan to do this, but desperate times call for desperate measures and I will just have to tell him we need a break from trying. He will understand so it isn't a big deal.

I sit in the waiting area until a nice lady called Tabitha calls me into the consultation room. She explains to me that I have two options, the Depo-Provera shot or the marina coil.

Weighing up the options, I feel the coil is better as it will not be something, I have to inject every three months. I lay down on the doctor's chair/bed and she advises me that this will be uncomfortable. Seeing as not too long ago I took strong painkillers though; this will minimise the pain.

Twenty minutes later, I am free to go. Yikes, she wasn't wrong, it was painful and uncomfortable. I send Corey a text explaining that we need to talk about my condition when he gets home later and then go about my mission.

I make my way to the Barasti Beach Bar, which is notoriously known amongst all tourists. If James claims he is on 'holiday', this is one of the first places to check. Bingo. He is sitting on a chair overlooking the ocean with a beer and a sandwich. Time to make the first move. I glide towards him and say, "Is this seat taken?" He looks up and smirks at me. Off to a good start.

"Well, hello there, trouble, no not at all please join me!"

"So, as you are on holiday, I had a feeling you would be here, beer in hand. Gosh I'm a genius! Would you be a gentleman and buy a lady a drink? I would love an aperol spritz." She has dived right in there with the charm, how predictable.

"Of course, how rude of me. One moment, darling, I seem to have temporarily forgotten my manners." I watch him as he strides over to the bar, I know he cannot resist our spark, so I'm confident this plan will work. To be honest, I am actually pretty excited about this endeavour…girl has still got it.

I wonder as I wait for her large aperol spritz, how long does she think she can resist my charm? Yes, she is extremely charming, but I am one step ahead and I know I charm harder than anyone. She is definitely a good contender though; I do have some competition. She probably thinks I will crack first, let's see about that shall we missy! Her drink is sitting on the bar counter now and I stride right back over to the table. "Here you go, my sweetheart. Don't drink it too fast now…we have more catching up to do."

"You know, James, I forgot how many pet names you come out with in one sitting, it's refreshing to hear such originality coming out of your mouth again." I can't hold back my laughter; her wit never seems to fail her.

"Ha-ha! You got me there, but what were you expecting? I think you know me pretty well by now. I am quite disappointed you forgot one of my main redeeming features so quickly!" she bites her lip and grins. Damn, she looks good.

"Well, James, the truth is, I could never forget such imperative information, I am only teasing you of course which you should already be used to." I gulp and take a huge swig of my beer. Looks like I need a top up.

"So, Cam, do tell me what is so fascinating about Dubai that you have decided to reside here permanently? Apart from the obvious reasons concerning the weather."

"I am glad you asked. Well, as briefly mentioned before, I met someone out here. He is lovely and he does make me happy but these days, I do find myself daring to think about the possibilities should I become single again. What about you? Do you have a special lady back in London? I would love to hear the details!" Of course, I need to divulge in excruciating detail that I am single and haven't found the one so she can put herself in my lane.

"Well, that is lovely to hear that you found someone but forgive me if I'm wrong, friend to friend, daring to imagine your life without him is dangerous territory. Do you have anyone in particular on your mind? Sadly, I am not married off yet. I haven't felt strongly about someone for a while now. You know, when you find a true connection with someone and it is like a fire burning deep inside, it is hard to top that." Ouch, I just felt a small fire burning in my private parts, is he talking about me? Smart move Mr, smart move. Nonetheless, I try to ignore the tingle and the sudden wetness now infiltrating my underwear and keep a poker face. Shit, he's made me cream my pants and he's not even touched me.

"Yes, I know what you mean, I have been there a couple times in life. It is hard to forget that kind of passion for someone. Fancy another drink? Oh, and for the record, I don't think I've ever heard you refer to me as a friend but hey, circumstances change don't they!" She is definitely hurt about the friend card I just threw at her; the look of annoyance is written all over her face and it is priceless. At least this proves she doesn't enjoy the thought of us being just friends.

"Oh Cam, I would love another beer, thanks darl." He knows for sure now based on my reaction that the thought of us being friends bothers me, for fucks sake, why do women allow their emotions to get the better of them? For that comment James, I urge you to go fuck yourself. A quick recovery is needed, so I reach over to grab his glass giving him an eyeful. His semi can be seen through the gaps in the table and so some of my control is restored.

A few more drinks are necked, and we find ourselves a tiny bit tipsy. Oh no, Camilla, this is not good for you because you get ten times hornier when you have been drinking. Shit oh shit, James is looking even sexier than he did twenty minutes ago. Pull yourself together, or actually, maybe I should seduce him? The chemistry is very apparent between us and he has definitely been flirting with the idea since he met me those years ago. Fuck it, time to get that semi of his, a bit harder.

"So, James, it is getting a bit late now, want to see the sunset on the beach? It is breath-taking, honestly!"

"You know what love, yes I would like that, haven't really paid the sunset much mind since being here, I'm following you!" *I wonder if the sunset is as breath-taking as her*, I think to myself as I follow behind her enjoying the view. James and I stroll along the beach until we end up at my favourite secluded part of the beach. We take a seat on the sand and stare up at the sun as it sets. The warm Dubai air still penetrating our skin. I steal a quick glance at him to see if he is watching it, and to my surprise, he is zoned out staring straight at it. I am glad he is appreciating this the way I imagined, it's always nice when you are with a man who can enjoy the likes of a sunset. I decide to turn it up a peg or two and shift a bit closer, laying my head on his shoulder to see if he flinches. Of course, he doesn't, he is completely captured in the moment and doesn't push me away. Excellent. I knew he wanted me. I give him a cheeky grin, and say, "I may be completely out of line here, but the water is so inviting especially at night, I tend to swim most evenings when it is quieter, fancy joining me this time?" Oh my god, James, mate, you have to take it easy, you already got caught up in the moment with the sunset and letting her rest her head on your shoulder! Fuck me, she's already taking her clothes off. My will power has completely disintegrated into thin air.

I decided to undress right there in front of him, because let's face it, his will power is non-existent just by looking at his expression. I am down to my underwear now and as I walk towards the ocean, my back facing him, off comes my underwear, now I am totally naked. Game on detective. "You coming in or what?" He hesitates for a second but then thirty seconds after that, he's taking off his shorts and his t-shirt, fancy that, he was already commando. Wow, that's a turn on. His growing erection is now on show for all to see and I have to say I am biting my lip involuntarily. He runs towards me and lifts me over his shoulder, throws me into the water and I giggle.

"Never would have pictured this as the first time we both see each other naked but it's definitely better, thanks for not chickening out!"

"Well, it seems you enticed me, well done, Cam, very good show you put on there!" He smirks and I melt a little bit, I want to take this to the next level so I splash his face playfully and move closer to him, putting my arms around his neck. I feel his hard-on pressing against my warm opening, he wants it too, time to kiss him. I lean in for the kiss and to my surprise, he grabs my face and returns my kiss with such passion I cannot wait any longer to feel his cock inside me. I wrap my legs around him and in one thrusting motion, he fills me up. I gasp at the feeling. We move in time with each other and it feels so good that my nails are digging into his soft but muscular back. It has been a long time coming. "For fucks sake, Cam, you feel incredible, why are you so sexy dammit!" hearing this, I moan even harder and this in turn pushes him over the edge and he picks up his pace. I have already cum twice but luckily, he didn't notice due to the water that surrounds us and then he finishes, letting out a slight groan. Once we both catch our breath again, we laugh. Also, once I catch my breath, I realise that I have just cheated on Corey. What a pickle I am in now! Fuuuck…

Me being the ridiculous cat mum that I am, had organised a wedding for Bubbles and her cat lover/boyfriend. Forgetting all about it during my explosive reunion with James, I hate myself for it. The cheating and the forgetting of the wedding. Nevertheless, after our night at the beach, fucking in the ocean, I ended up inviting him to the ceremony, at my house, in my garden, with my boyfriend. Another one of my marvellous plans. However, in light of my actions, it is imperative that I remain neutral and act like there is no carnal urge to jump on James every time he gives me that cheeky wink. God, I am screwed. Another day in the lift of Camilla.

The wedding day has come around all to quickly and Bubbles and Sam are like two lovesick puppies as the saying goes because I don't think one has been made for their kind yet. Bastards. The dress code is all white because you know, it's classic and everyone owns some white clothing. Hold up a minute, have I gone absolutely mental? A fucking cat wedding. They don't even know what this is they're just sitting there licking each other and chasing their tales. Fuck, maybe there is an underlining reason for this. Maybe, I want to get married? I really think I have hit rock bottom, but I cannot cancel this ridiculous event because I am in it now. I am just placing some food down for both cats to chow down on and I feel a familiar hand on my shoulder. "I have to say, this is a first. Haven't been to a wedding in years and my first one this year is a pair of cats. I think I've seen it all now!" I snarl at the remark and although I agree it's stupid, the only person allowed to have this opinion is me. So, fuck off, James.

"Hahaha, you are too funny, but this is a serious matter actually. Any two people, or animals, should be allowed to have a special day! You may have just lost your invite with that attitude, Mr!" Well, that may have come across a bit strong, but I think I am just angry about the fact he has come into my life again and once again turned my brain into mush. Sarcasm was definitely necessary though and I stand by it.

"Wow, okay, look, darling, I didn't mean to offend was only joking...so where is this lovely fella of yours then? I am dying to meet him. Don't worry, I will act like we're just old friends and didn't just fuck in the ocean last night. Scouts honour." He's such a prick sometimes, I want to sit on his face.

"This way, you absolute moron." As we stroll over to meet my wonderful fella, and let's face it, I don't deserve him anymore, I grab a large glass of wine and gulp it down in an effort to distract myself from the looming disaster that is this day.

"Corey, honey, I want to introduce you to an old friend from London. He is a carpenter by trade (and a scheming undercover copper who is out to arrest me), James, meet Corey."

"It's always a pleasure to meet anyone from Camilla's hometown, how do you do, sir? Thank you for coming to this event, I know the cats really appreciate the turn out." Ah, Corey, ever the gentleman, I am going to hell.

"Nice to meet you too, Corey, you have a beautiful home and the weather is incredible. Kind of bummed I have to go back to shitty English weather again soon!"

"Oh no, when are you leaving? You should stay for the rest of the weekend, please it will be our pleasure, wouldn't it, Cam love?" Erm, no, it would not be our pleasure. What a terrible idea but how can I say no without looking suspicious?

"Yes, of course, James, we would be delighted to have you as our guest this weekend, the guest bedroom is all yours!"

Although watching my beloved Bubbles tie the knot with her now husband brought a tear to my eye, I could not fully concentrate, and my mind was all over the place. What was I going to do, I know I am a sensational actress (it comes with the escorting), I felt so deeply guilty that two men who I have extremely strong feelings for, were effectively being pawns in my love story. I had to make sure James leaves this weekend and that his suspicions towards me cease. I have to forget about the love we made and lock it away in my deepest darkest thoughts box. My life was here now with Corey.

We all sit at the dinner table sharing wine and the two men are sharing manly stories, getting on famously. I have to hand it to James; he has played out this other life of a carpenter very well and it is so convincing. The deceitful parasite. Okay, yes, I am a hypocrite, but you know what, I am only human, and three-ways are one of my specialities. No, not time to make sexual jokes here. I need to focus. We are on our third bottle of wine, so it is safe to say we are all feeling the effects. I am trying my best to remain a mute during this exasperating conversation but oh no, they wouldn't let me would they. "Camilla, honey, James is a very funny man, I like him very much. How did you two come to meet again?" Why would you do this to me Corey, why?

"It is quite a funny story actually; you see I was in the airport in France for a work-related trip and I slipped over, and James decided to help me up from the floor. Our first encounter was brief, but I bumped into him again in London and we had a coffee and got chatting. Now, we are great friends and that is basically it honey."

"Yeah, that sounds about right. Poor old Cam had a wet patch all over her backside, it was hard not to laugh to be honest, Corey! Bumping into her in London was such a coincidence but are good friends now. They do say everything happens for a reason, don't they?" Hmmm, and what reason is this trip to Dubai, other than to incarcerate me?

"Well, guys, I am going to hit the hay now, the wine has definitely got to me. Thank you, James, for joining us. My love, are you coming to bed right away or?"

"No, not yet honey, I have to finish off some work in the office I didn't complete today due to the wedding. I will join you in a couple of hours, okay. James, you know where you will be sleeping? Cam can show you to your room."

"Fab, this way, James." As we make our way down the hall, the silence is deafening, and you could cut the sexual tension with a knife. We approach the guest bedroom door and as I go to open it, James grabs my arm and swivels me round, so I am facing him. He strokes my cheek and then kisses me, a deep carnal kiss which I was hoping and praying he did not do. Unable to control myself, I jump up, wrap my legs around him and he opens the door, in one swift motion, he throws me onto the bed. Our hands our all over each other and his erection is throbbing, I gasp, pull down his shorts and pants and start sucking his dick aggressively, teasing it with my tongue. He moans as I look directly into his eyes, he looks like he is about to cum, so he stops me, bends me over the bed and pounds me senseless. What am I doing? Why is this happening? I cannot seem to resist this man and it is dangerous. I suddenly realise what we are doing and stop him. "We cannot do this, I have a boyfriend, you have to leave first thing tomorrow morning and please do not come back." I storm out of the room with tear filled eyes because in that moment, I realised I was in love with two men at the same time.

Oh fuck, why does this woman have so much control over me? She drives me beyond sanity. I am supposed to be investigating her, not fucking her. Wait, fucking doesn't sound right, it felt like we were making love both times, the level of passion ignited between us, it has to be more. I am in huge trouble; I am in love with Camilla Jones. I don't even wait until the morning; I slip out as soon as possible because waiting until the morning seemed far too long.

I go back to my hotel, grab my bags and get on the first flight home. Camilla will just have to be a suspect I leave behind, and I will figure out the how to do that as soon as I have landed.

Chapter Seventeen

I wake up, in bed, Corey beside me. I was in and out of sleep all night because I could not fathom what I had done to him. I would never usually cheat, that is one of the worst possible crimes to commit in a relationship. That being said, I would now be branded a cheater and I felt utterly ashamed. Here is this man, lying next to me, he supports me and loves me, he is truly wonderful, and I was so happy with him that I left my life behind in London. Now, I have jeopardised it all for an old flame who it seems I haven't truly let go of. How does an escort, whose main focus in life is to have sex without any relationship ties, end up falling for two men? I don't know what to do. My head is telling me to stay here with Corey, he is so good for me and he isn't a copper who is at risk of finding out what I used to do. That was the entire reason why James and I never pursued anything further, at the time he didn't know that I knew what he was really doing and he still doesn't know that I know, so nothing has changed. I wonder if he has left the house yet, I hope he has. I couldn't bear to look at his face again.

Unable to feign my curiosity, I get out of bed and go down the hall to check. I cannot help myself. I open the door ever so gently as not to wake him, but to my unfortunate surprise, he was gone. I was relieved but also extremely disappointed. I actually felt a pang of pain rush to my heart. For the second time, I had lost him. As I process this, I slowly walk back down the hall and into the bathroom. I sit down in the shower, and I cry.

Overwhelmed with feelings of guilt, I try to hide my feelings and avoid Corey as much as possible that morning. I had to get out of the house. I walk down to the beach hut, ordered a large coffee and stared out into the sea. I had to make an important decision, do I tell Corey and risk losing him too? Or do I forget James for the last time and continue my happy life here? As much as honesty is usually the best policy, I have lived my life lying to the people I care the most about, so I choose to move forward. My indiscretion would be the only indiscretion in my relationship with Corey because let's face it, although he deserves better, I do love him, and this is my life now. James Splinter is a thing of the past. Before I let him go, I walk over to the edge of the sea, sit down and let the waves drown my feet, I close my eyes, remember the magical night we shared here and as soon as I open them, he disappears.

Touch down in London, I, James Splinter have fucked up for the last time. Whilst I was on my way back from Dubai, I realised that I had to quit my job as a detective inspector. Though getting the bad guy was my first love, I met a second who I loved more. I hate to admit it, but I cannot work on an investigation that may or may not implicate the woman I love. You may call me crazy, a complete bell-end for quitting a job for a woman, but to be honest, I have never loved anyone before, and this is just not worth it. I have to let her live her life in Dubai, with her boyfriend even if it is killing me softly just like the Fugees. See what I mean? I just quoted a song title to explain how I was feeling, this has to be real. I had to do this quickly, so as soon as I get to the station, I hand in my resignation. It isn't all bad, I have that carpenter business still, so I can just focus on building tables and chairs for the rest of my life. Sawing away my pain and anguish for the decision I have just made.

A year goes by and I am enjoying my job. I genuinely feel such relief that I am no longer putting myself or anyone else at risk. Also, on my tab, I may as well add that I have met someone new. This cute little lady called Jodie. She is a single mum and we met when she purchased some furniture from my carpentry store. She is funny and kind and beautiful. I never actually thought of myself as a father, but her 10-year-old daughter Penny is delightful. She is starting secondary school in September as she turns 11 in April, so no doubt the hormones will be kicking in way too soon, but though I am not her father, that is okay because we have become close nonetheless. I take her to the park, for hot chocolate and we even play football together. I can safely say, I may be on my way to loving again.

Back in Dubai, a year after James was here, I am happily married, yes married to Corey. Due to my endometriosis, we decided to adopt a son, a 10-year-old boy called Damien. He was very shy to begin with, which we thought was normal due to him being adopted. However, we could not be more content with the little family we had now created. Damien and Bubbles were thick as thieves, I could say I was jealous because first she dumps me for her cat husband and now her focus has shifted to my son, but I am not. I am ecstatic that she has warmed up to him the same way he has warmed to her. After all, she was and will always be my first child. The fact that he was starting secondary school soon was terrifying. He turns 11 in a couple of months in June and we have a huge birthday bash planned for him. There will be a huge bouncy castle, all his friends from primary school will be there. It was going to be a blast. It will be especially important because it will be his first birthday with us as our son and it genuinely feels like we won the lottery. Who would have thought I would have a husband and a son? I certainly wanted this for myself but didn't think it would actually happen.

Two months later…

So, you know how I was bragging about how smug I was with my happy life with my son and Corey? Well, this is a turn out for the books, since James's visit, I haven't been able to get my mind off him and I felt so incredibly guilty about our rendezvous that I came clean to Corey. He was obviously devastated but it was eating me up inside and I couldn't bear it anymore. He gave me another month to arrange a home for Damien and I back in London, I also had to enrol him into a secondary school starting September. I searched for a two-bedroom flat in Central London, I came to the conclusion that Holborn was a nice place to live, yes I know the prices are extortionate but as Corey and I are finalising our divorce, I am entitled to half of his money which I know I don't deserve but that's what happens to married couples. Due to this, I can buy this flat upfront and not have to worry about rent payments. I call the estate agent and make the international wire transfer along with all of the signed paperwork. Once I get the confirmation, I arrange to pick up the keys in two days when my flight is booked. Damien, being so used to the hot climate here in Dubai will certainly miss it and I can assure him I will too. Bless him, he doesn't understand why he and mummy are leaving and it does worry me that I have scarred him for life. I am determined not to fuck this up though and make sure he is well taken care of even if I am a single mum. I take a swig of my glass of Merlot and start looking at schools. Regent High School looks like it could be decent, it is mixed and not too far from the flat. I decide to pick this one and start the enrolling process, there we are done. I then pour myself another glass of wine and take a deep breath. It's time for a fresh start, but this time it's not just me and Bubbles this time. Of course, she is coming with me back to London, cat marriages are hardly binding, and she will get over it!

The day before Damien and I are off to our new life, I finish packing our suitcases. I give Mum and Dad a quick call to let them know when we land so they can pick us up from Heathrow. As you can probably imagine, they are ecstatic for our return. Once the call is finished, I tuck Damien into bed and set an alarm for when we have to leave. Whilst he is sleeping, I say my final goodbyes to Corey. He looks at me with that look of disappointment I have been receiving ever since I told him I cheated but being the lovely man he is, he forces a half smile and says, "Cam, please look after yourself and Damien. I am sorry things turned out this way for us but I want you to know that I will always care deeply for you and our son. He is just better off with you in London where you can give him the attention he deserves. Have a safe flight the both of you and let me know when you have landed." He then gives me a hug and a kiss on the forehead, I try to stifle my urge to cry but a single teardrop still runs down my cheek.

Chapter Eighteen

We land at around 12:00 pm in the afternoon at Heathrow, as soon as we get through customs, I send a text to Corey and give my mum a ring to see where they are. "Hi, darling, we are just waiting outside the Costa, see you shortly." Being back in London gives me a huge sense of nostalgia. This is where I spent most of my life including the days where I was an escort. Wow, thinking about my past and what my life is now, the two just do not collaborate at all. Funny that. I think for a moment, what would happen if Damien found out somehow what I used to do and he left me out of shame. It is unimaginable to think how your child would react to such revelations but I do still stand my ground and think that women should be able to have such careers and not be shamed by society for it. That being said, I am now a mother and that kind of lifestyle is fully behind me now. Damien has met Mum and Dad before, so when he sees them, he does run up to them and give them a cuddle. I slowly catch up, suitcases in either hand and Bubbles in her cat carrier being carried by the nice gentleman working for the airport staff. Luckily, my father strolls over to him and takes over the carrier and Bubbles remembering who he is starts bouncing with delight. "Hello, love, how was your flight? The little one has grown so fast this past year where does the time go? Let's get a coffee and hit the road, we are dying to see your new place!"

"Thanks, Dad, I know please do not remind me, he is growing too quickly in my opinion. Sure, I cannot wait to see it myself, the photos were decent and I had a virtual tour so I have an idea but nothing like seeing it in the flesh."

We are heading down the motorway, I have wound down the windows so I can feel the summer air and so that Damien feels it too. "Mummy, how long until it starts to rain?" I chuckle at his humour; he is a witty lad.

"Let's hope not for at least the next hour, darling?" I scoff playfully. I am so anxious to see where we will be living and this anxiety keeps growing as we approach the street. I hope the neighbours are friendly and that Damien can make friends. My revere is interrupted as we stop at a halt in front of the block. "Up and out, darling, here we are! Let's get your bags shall we!" My mum says with glee. She is still as excitable as ever and I secretly missed that. We all get out of the car and the estate sales manager is waiting at the entrance. I leave my parents to unload the bags and walk over to her. Debra I think her name was. "Camilla? Welcome to your new home! Isn't this exciting? Come now, I will show you the place it's just over here." I chose a ground floor flat because this meant that Damien had access to the garden. I follow Debra and we stop outside flat number 3. Appealing red door to start which is cool because I love the colour red for obvious reasons. She puts the key in and turns it clockwise, as we enter, I see that the part furnished items are all in their rightful places. Oven, washing machine, even a fridge/freezer. We do another tour of each room and to my relief it was as expected and I already felt at home. My parents and Damien are now standing behind

Debra and I in the lounge. "What do you think, kiddo? Your room is the one on the left there go have a look!"

He listens and gives the room the once over. Both rooms are large and I also have an ensuite in the main bedroom. There is a walk in shower which is to die for and a sizeable bathtub in the main bathroom which I am already picturing with candles and some radox bubble bath. Once we are all acquainted with the place, Debra hands me the keys and wishes us bon voyage. Now, we cannot unpack just yet because we are expecting a delivery around 3:00 pm with the sofa, tv, beds and wardrobes. Whilst we wait we order some pizza from Dominos and sit on the floor in a circle, a bit like we are in a cult and about to sacrifice a goat. I am just putting a piece of chicken supreme pizza into my mouth when the door goes. The delivery guys are right on schedule, perfect.

The next few hours, we spend putting things together whilst Dad pops out for a food shop. We have a lot more homely touches to make but we have the basics in place for now. Bubbles is exploring her new home, probably comparing it to how small it must feel to the big house in Dubai but I am sure she will warm to it because she lived in a flat with me beforehand. I sit down on the sofa and gesture for Damien to accompany me. "What do you think, handsome? Do you like it here so far?"

"It's okay, mummy, just getting used to it and not seeing Daddy, it's sad he couldn't come with us"

"I know, honey, I am so sorry he isn't here but don't worry, you will still speak to him every day I promise!"

"Thank you, mummy, I love you."

My heart melts and I hold him tight. "I love you too, sweetie."

The next day, waking up in my new flat, the sun is shining through gaps in the blinds. I didn't sleep the best but that is normal for a first night in a new place. I hope Damien slept okay and with that in mind, I step out of bed and make my way to his room. I poke my head round the door and see he is up and about. "Knock, knock, how did you sleep?"

He hesitates before answering, poor little lamb, "Fine, mummy, the sun woke me up! Can we go for a walk today?"

"Of course, buddy, we have to explore the area, see what we can find! I will whip us up some breakfast and then we can get ready." I cannot forget to feed the real princess of the family too so I pour a generous portion of Whiskas into a bowl and place it by Bubbles' bed. She emerges from underneath the dining table and sashays over. Such a sassy puss that one.

I am showered and ready whilst Damien is struggling to decide what shoes to wear, you'd think I was the one fussing about with shoes but he finds his blue converse and starts to tie his shoelaces accordingly. We both give Bubbles a goodbye kiss and head down the street. I of course know the area quite well being a Londoner myself but Damien has only ever lived in Dubai, lucky sod if you ask me. Watching him take in his surroundings is quite delightful and I remind myself how fortunate I am to have him. My endometriosis is under control and I have accepted that whether or not I gave birth to Damien or not he is my baby. We come up to a high street and I am dying for an ice cream and I know he is too. It is 30 degrees here in London today would you believe it? I certainly fucking don't but here we are, sweating and enjoying the results of possible climate change. There is an ice cream shop just to the left and I waste no time in ordering myself a pistachio and vanilla combo and a chocolate and caramel combo for the boy. Goodness, he has such a sweet tooth, better keep an eye on him so he doesn't get early onset diabetes.

We take our ice cream cones and head for the park. He sits beside me on the bench, and we are both in complete silence whilst demolishing our sweet treats. I wish I could read his mind and see what he is thinking but the truth is he is probably thinking of absolutely nothing, oh to be a kid again. My mind takes me back to when I first started taking clients on, Barbara being my Madam certainly kept me busy. I have come across some really messed up individuals in my time and I giggle to myself. The thing is, I don't miss it. The independence was great but now I have my son I have dived right into the deep end of motherhood. I guess there are mixed reviews on what a woman should be doing with her life and to be honest I do not regret any of my decisions apart from one. This is going to sound so cliché but fuck it. I missed out on an opportunity with that James Splinter and I know it.

Sadly, it was not achievable at the time, what with him being an undercover detective in the prostitution world. I do wonder though what it would have been like if he was actually a carpenter and I gave it a go. I would have most likely had to quit my escorting and stuck it out at that boring office, having Bobby trying his luck with me whilst being fully aware that I was now in a relationship. Hypothetically speaking because of course that is not what the situation is at all. Damien brings me back to the real world and asks where we are going next. We have to pop into town to get some more bits for the house, like decorative bits to make it look pretty with a touch of 11-year-old.

We get a bunch of bits from next homeware and I treat Damien to a new coat. He will need a warmer one once winter kicks in. we give my parents a call because there is no way all this stuff will fit in a cab and they have a massive people carrier car now as to be more 'child friendly' which I admit benefits me greatly! We pull up to the block and Mum and Dad help us with our bags, once settled, it is starting to feel like the flat has its own personality which was the goal.

The next couple of months are spent going to the seaside in Southend, visiting the parks, museums and bonding time with the family. September is creeping in a couple of weeks, so I put my mum head into gear getting his school uniform prepared, his stationery, backpack etc. I am having mini anxiety attacks the whole time worrying way too much about the things I cannot change, like the fact he has to go to school, he has to grow up. I have missed most of his toddler years, so the thought of him being a teenager in a couple years does raise one's blood pressure. He is not worried at all because of cause the sheer ignorance of children is bliss and I am envious. I give my mum a call to see if she can offer some words of wisdom having raised me. We sit on the sofa with a cuppa tea (no wine for me for a change). "Mum, I realise this is all new to me but does it get easier being a full-time mum? Granted I am a single mum, at least you had Dad!"

"Honey, you had Corey in the beginning sure but it doesn't mean you cannot do this on your own, you also have us by your side to help you! He is a wonderful little boy and I know it is a worry that he is going to big school in two weeks but all kids do grow up eventually. Sometimes before their time but you just need to take each day as it comes! I raised you and you came out okay!" She chuckles to herself at her humour.

"Thanks, mum, yes I know I am overthinking things but I just don't want to fuck this up!"

"Language, dear!"

"Whoops, sorry, mum, forgot a grown lady is not allowed to swear in front of her mother." I tease. We smile at each other and she gives me a warm sticky hug, it's still warm outside but I am enjoying the embrace.

The dreadful day has come, 1 September. I am making sure Damien has his things ready and we set off to his new school. He is actually buzzing with excitement, makes one of us. As we approach the gate we see large groups of kids dressed in their uniform, so many children in one place. Hold on a minute, I am acting like I haven't been to fucking school before. I guess it's just a different experience when it is a mother overseeing all of this mania. I reach out to grab Damien as an attempt to pull him away but hold back because my fears certainly should never be evident to my kid and what am I worried about? It's not like I can home-school the poor guy, he wouldn't stand a chance! The bell chimes to alert all children to enter the building and find their school form group. "Mummy, it's time for me to go I think. Don't worry, I will be okay! I love you."

"Yes, it seems that is the case sweetie, alright off you go, enjoy yourself! I will pick you up at 3:30 pm, love you too!" and with that he scurries off. My heart starts beating super-fast, too early for wine, shit. What do I do? I go find the nearest Starbucks and order a coffee instead. Oh sod off, I know what you are thinking, caffeine is the worst thing to put into your body when you are having anxiety but you know what, I've had worse inside me and the pun is definitely intended. The day goes by so slowly but 3:30 pm approaches and I am outside the gate ready and waiting for my baby boy to exit those daunting double doors. About 30 kids at once usher their way out of the doors and then in amongst them I see Damien's little face. He is smiling so wide I think he must have had a better day than I thought! The crowd disperses and there I see it, my boy and a young girl next to him giggling away. Ah, is this a girlfriend already or is she just a friend? I am dying to find out. I approach them both and put my hand out to introduce myself to his little girl pal.

"Hi! I am Camilla, Damien's mum, nice to meet you. What is your name, sweetheart?" She grabs my hand gladly and strongly I might add, damn she is a firecracker I can tell. "Hello! My name is Penny. Damien and I have decided to be form buddies!"

"Yes, mum, that is right! Penny is in my form group; we are going to be the best of friends!" Got to love the innocence of children don't you, meet someone once and become best pals without all the bullshit adult politics out there. I like her.

"That is great, the both of you! Penny we would love to have you round sometime, Damien loves to play football in the garden!" She nods enthusiastically and then her mum approaches. She is a very pretty lady.

"Hi, I am Damien's mum, Camilla, your Penny here is quite lovely! What is your name?"

"Hello love, nice to meet you both! My name is Jodie."

127

Chapter Nineteen

So, Penny has started school and keeps telling Jodie and I about her new best mate Damien. She speaks very highly of him despite their ripe age of 11. It is very cute I must admit, maybe he's her boyfriend? Well, either way, I will be meeting the young chap tonight as he has organised a playdate with the mother. Jodie has some errands to run so on this warm but breezy Wednesday evening, I have offered to drop her off to the house. They are going to play football together. I jump in the car and Penny slides in next to me. She is high off excitement and I kind of wish I were that fucking excited myself! Since I left the detective job and focused my time on the carpentry business, I have often wondered if I was missing out on that kind of lifestyle. Busy, always on the go solving cases. When you do that kind of job it is hard to compare it to. Having said that, I am happy with Jodie and her kid is a darling.

I pull up at Rover Lane just off of Holborn, this is where the block of flats are I think. I check the address in my sat nav and it is right, Flat 3, Rover Lane. "Right, princess, we are here! Go grab your bits from the back seat." We both stroll to the front communal entrance; press number 3 and the buzzer lets us in. I knock on the door and cannot believe who opens it. Camilla fucking Jones. I am in shock because the woman in front of me is with child and in London. The shock is also written all over her face for a short while but she dismisses this and leads with that cheeky grin. Oh boy, I am in trouble.

"Hi, you must be Penny's mother's boyfriend? I'm Camilla."

"Hello, there, yes that's me, James is the name. just dropping Penny off as her mother is busy."

"Makes complete sense, why don't you come in for a cuppa and we let the kids go have some fun outside?" Fuck me, who would have thought it? I didn't think I would ever see her again but here we are and I am intrigued to see how she has wound up here, with a kid on her own.

I sit down and she puts a cup in front of me whilst grabbing her own. She looks at me and still I find it hard to speak. Please don't let her know she still has this effect on me. "So, last time I saw you, we were in Dubai and you were with that Corey fella. Where did the child come from? Even I know babies don't grow up that fast!" Good start.

"Well, you certainly have picked up on that one fast, well done for your amazing observation! When you left, I was pretty torn up. Thought it was best to move forward with Corey as he was my partner, so we got married and adopted Damien at age 10. With my endometriosis, I can still conceive but it is hard to carry and can result in miscarriages. So, I thought what better than to bring a young child as wonderful as he is into our lives. Was the best decision I ever made. Sadly though, I couldn't deal with the guilt of what happened between you and me anymore, so I came clean to Corey and we decided it was best to divorce and for me to move here and start fresh. Was not expecting to see you obviously, especially as the chauffer for my son's playdate!"

Wow, she told him about us. This is also unexpected, so I have to think of a better way to respond. I take a gulp of my tea and go for it. "Well, I can safely say I was not expecting to see you again, and even more so in these circumstances. When I left Dubai, I ran into Jodie and Penny at my carpentry workshop and we just hit it off, the three of us. Felt like it could be a good start to something new. Sorry to hear about your marriage ending because of what happened between us, it was never my intention. That being said, no need to live in the past now, so I guess we will be seeing a lot more of each other!"

"I guess so, this is going to be fun! No hard feelings right?"

"Of course not, darling, water under the bridge." The playdate comes to an end, hitting 7:00 pm, so myself and Penny make our departure and I cannot help but think this is a sign for a chance for Camilla and I to be friends. I'm kind of looking forward to it!

What the fuck just happened? Was James Splinter in my flat, in my face? You know when life just keeps hitting you with surprises and you think it better quit! After spending a few hours in his company again, I worry I will start feigning for him again, for a third time. Fucking hell, this just could not be any weirder. For the record, he seems happy with his little set up and I would never want to get in the way of that before you start calling me a homewrecker…but I am slightly jealous. This is okay though because it isn't about him and I, it is about the kids. I would rather have him in my life as a friend than nothing at all because honestly that seemed way harder when I think about it. Let's see how this goes. You never know what the future holds, so stay tuned.